The Shadow On The Dial, and Other Essays

Ambrose Bierce

Editor: S.O. Howes

Contents

THE SHADOW ON THE DIAL, AND OTHER ESSAYS

BY

Ambrose Bierce

Editor: S.O. Howes

A NOTE BY THE AUTHOR

IT WAS expected that this book would be included in my "Collected Works" now in course of publication, but unforeseen delay in the date of publication has made this impossible. The selection of its contents was not made by me, but the choice has my approval and the publication my authority.

AMBROSE BIERCE.
Washington, D. C. March 14. 1909.

PREFACE

THE note of prophecy! It sounds sharp and clear in many a vibrant line, in many a sonorous sentence of the essays herein collected for the first time. Written for various Californian journals and periodicals and extending over a period of more than a quarter of a century, these opinions and reflections express the refined judgment of one who has seen, not as through a glass darkly, the trend of events. And having seen the portentous effigy that we are making of the Liberty our fathers created, he has written of it in English that is the despair of those who, thinking less clearly, escape not the pitfalls of diffuseness and obscurity. For Mr. Bierce, as did Flaubert, holds that the right word is necessary for the conveyance of the right thought and his sense of word values rarely betrays him into error. But with an odd--I might almost say perverse--indifference to his own reputation, he has allowed these writings to lie fallow in the old files of papers, while others, possessing the knack of publicity, years later tilled the soil with some degree of success. President Hadley, of Yale University, before the Candlelight Club of Denver, January 8, 1900, advanced, as novel and original, ostracism as an effective punishment of social highwaymen. This address attracted widespread attention, and though Professor Hadley's remedy has not been generally adopted it is regarded as his own. Mr. Bierce wrote in "The Examiner," January 20, 1895, as follows: "We are plundered because we have no particular aversion to plunderers."

The 'predatory rich' (to use Mr. Stead's felicitous term) put their hands into our pockets because they know that, virtually, none of us will refuse to take their hands in our own afterwards, in friendly salutation. If notorious rascality entailed social outlawry the only rascals would be those properly--and proudly--belonging to the 'criminal class.'

Again, Edwin Markham has attracted to himself no little attention by advocating the application of the Golden Rule in temporal affairs as a cure for evils arising from industrial discontent In this he, too, has been anticipated. Mr. Bierce, writing in "The Examiner," March 25, 1894, said: "When a people would avert want and strife, or having them, would restore plenty and peace, this noble commandment offers the only means--all other plans for safety and relief are as vain as dreams, and as empty as the crooning of fools. And, behold, here it is: 'All things whatsoever ye would that men should do to you, do ye even so to them.'"

Rev. Charles M. Sheldon created a nine days' wonder, or rather a seven, by conducting for a week a newspaper as he conceived Christ would have done. Some years previously, June 28, 1896, to be exact, the author of these essays wrote: "That is my ultimate and determining test of right--'What, under the circumstances, would Christ have done?'--the Christ of the New Testament, not the Christ of the commentators, theologians, priests and parsons."

I am sure that Mr. Bierce does not begrudge any of these gentlemen the acclaim they have received by enunciating his ideas, and I mention the instances here merely to forestall the filing of any other claim to priority.

The essays cover a wide range of subjects, embracing among other things government, dreams, writers of dialect, and dogs, and always the author's point of view is fresh, original and non-Philistine. Whether one cares to agree with him or not, one will find vast entertainment in his wit that illuminates with lightning flashes all he touches. Other qualities I forbear allusion to, having already encroached too much upon the time of the reader.

S. O. HOWES.

THE SHADOW ON THE DIAL
I.

THERE is a deal of confusion and uncertainty in the use of the words "Socialist," "Anarchist," and "Nihilist." Even the '1st himself commonly knows with as little accuracy what he is as the rest of us know why he is. The Socialist believes that most human affairs should be regulated and managed by the State--the Government--that is to say, the majority. Our own system has many Socialistic features and the trend of republican government is all that way. The Anarchist is the kind of lunatic who believes that all crime is the effect of laws forbidding it--as the pig that breaks into the kitchen garden is created by the dog that chews its ear! The Anarchist favors abolition of all law and frequently belongs to an organization that secures his allegiance by solemn oaths and dreadful penalties. "Nihilism" is a name given by Turgenieff to the general body of Russian discontent which finds expression in antagonizing authority and killing authorities. Constructive politics would seem, as yet, to be a cut above the Nihilist's intelligence; he is essentially a destructionary. He is so diligently engaged in unweeding the soil that he has not given a thought to what he will grow there. Nihilism may be described as a policy of assassination tempered by reflections upon Siberia. American sympathy with it is the offspring of an unholy union between the tongue of a liar and the ear of a dupe.

Upon examination it will be seen that political dissent, when it takes any form more coherent than the mere brute dissatisfaction of a mind that does not know what it wants to want, finds expression in one of but two ways--in Socialism or in Anarchism. Whatever methods one may think will best substitute for a system gradually evolved from our needs and our natures a system existing only in the minds of dreamers, one is bound to choose between these two dreams. Yet such is the intellectual delinquency of many who most strenuously denounce the system that we have that we not infrequently find the same man advocating in one breath, Socialism, in the next, Anarchism. Indeed, few of these sons of darkness know that even as coherent dreams the two are incompatible. With Anarchy triumphant the Socialist would be a thousand years further from realization of his hope than he is today. Set up Socialism on a Monday and on Tuesday the country would be ***en fete***, gaily hunting down Anarchists. There would be little difficulty in trailing them, for they have not so much sense as a deer, which, running down the wind, sends its tell-tale fragrance on before.

Socialism and Anarchism are the two extremes of political thought; they are parts of the same dung, in the sense that the terminal points of a road are parts of the same road. Between them, about midway, lies the system that we have the happiness to endure. It is a "blend" of Socialism and Anarchism in about equal parts: all that is not one is the other. Everything serving the common interest, or looking to the welfare of the whole people, is socialistic in the strictest sense of the word as understood by the Socialist Whatever tends to private advantage or advances an individual or class interest at the expense of a public one, is anarchistic. Cooperation is Socialism; competition is Anarchism. Competition carried to its logical conclusion (which only cooperation prevents or can prevent) would leave no law in force no property possible no life secure.

Of course the words "cooperation" and "competition" are not here used in a merely industrial and commercial sense; they are intended to cover the whole field of human activity. Two voices singing a duet--that is cooperation--Socialism. Two voices singing each a different tune and trying to drown each other--that is competition--Anarchism: each is a law unto itself--that is to say, it is lawless. Everything that ought to be done the Socialist hopes to do by associated endeavor, as an army wins battles; Anarchism is socialistic in its means only: by cooperation it tries to render cooperation impossible--combines to kill combination. Its method says to its purpose: "Thou fool!"

II.

Everything foretells the doom of authority. The killing of kings is no new industry; it is as ancient as the race. Always and everywhere persons in high place have been the assassin's prey. We have ourselves lost three Presidents by murder, and will doubtless lose many another before the book of American history is closed. If anything is new in this activity of the regicide it is found in the choice of victims. The contemporary "avenger" slays, not the merely great, but the good and the inoffensive--an American President who had struck the chains from millions of slaves; a Russian Czar who against the will and work of his own powerful nobles had freed their serfs; a French President from whom the French people had received nothing but good; a powerless Austrian Empress, whose weight of sorrows touched the world to tears; a blameless Italian King beloved of his people; such is a part of the recent record of the regicide whose every entry is a tale of infamy unrelieved by one circumstance of justice, decency or good intention.

And the great Brazilian liberator died in exile.

This recent uniformity of malevolence in the choice of victims is not without significance. It points unmistakably to two facts: first, that the selections are made, not by the assassins themselves, but by some central control inaccessible to individual preference and unaffected by the fortunes of its instruments; second, that there is a constant purpose to manifest an antagonism, not to any individual ruler, but to rulers; not to any system of government, but to Government. It is a war, not upon those in authority, but upon Authority. The issue is defined, the alignment made, the battle set: Chaos against Order, Anarchy against Law.

M. Vaillant, the French gentleman who lacked a "good opinion of the law," but was singularly rich in the faith that by means of gunpowder and flying nails humanity could be brought into a nearer relation with reason, righteousness and the will of God, is said to have been nearly devoid of a nose. Of this affliction M. Vaillant made but slight account, as was natural, seeing that but for a brief season did he need even so much of nose as remained to him. Yet before its effacement by premature disruption of his own petard it must have had a certain value to him--he would not wantonly have renounced it; and had he foreseen its extinction by the bomb the iron views of that controversial device would probably have been denied expression. Albeit (so say the scientists) doomed to eventual elimination from the scheme of being, and to the Anarchist even now something of an accusing conscience, the nose is indubitably an excellent thing in man.

This brings us to consideration of the human nose as a measure of human happiness--not the size of it, but its numbers; its frequent or infrequent occurrence upon the human face. We have grown so accustomed to the presence of this feature that we take it as a matter of course; its absence is one of the most notable phenomena of our observation--"an occasion long to be remembered," as the society reporter hath it Yet "abundant testimony showeth" that but two or three centuries ago noseless men and women were so common all over Europe as to provoke but little comment when seen and (in their disagreeable way) heard They abounded in all the various walks of life: there were honored burgomasters without noses, wealthy merchants, great scholars, artists, teachers. Amongst the humbler classes nasal destitution was almost as frequent as pecuniary--in the humblest of all the most common of all. Writing in the thirteenth century, Salsius mentions the retainers and servants of certain Suabian noblemen as having hardly a whole ear among them--for until a comparatively recent period man's tenure of his ears was even more precarious than that of his nose. In 1436, when a Bavarian woman, Agnes Bemaurian, wife of Duke Albert the Pious, was dropped off the bridge at Prague, she persisted in rising to the surface and trying to escape; so the executioner gave himself the trouble to put a long pole into her hair and hold her under. A contemporary account of the matter hints that her disorderly behavior at so solemn a moment was due to the pain caused by removal of her nose; but as her execution was by order of her own father it seems more probable that "the extreme penalty of the law" was not imposed. Without a doubt, though, possession of a nose was an uncommon (and rather barren) distinction in those days among "persons designated to assist the executioner," as the condemned were civilly called. Nor, as already said, was it any too common among persons not as yet consecrated to that service: "Few," says Salsius, "have two noses, and many have none."

Man's firmer grasp upon his nose in this our day and generation is not altogether due to invention of the handkerchief. The genesis and development of his right to his own nose have been accompanied with a corresponding advance in the possessory rights all along the line of his belongings--his ears, his fingers and toes, his skin, his bones, his wife and her young, his clothes and his labor--everything that is (and that once was not) his. In Europe and America today these things can not be taken away from even the humblest and poorest without somebody wanting to "know the reason why." In every decade the nation that is most powerful upon the seas incurs voluntarily a vast expense of blood and treasure in suppressing a slave trade which in no way is injurious to her interests, nor to the interests of any but the slaves.

So "Freedom broadens slowly down," and today even the lowliest incapable of all Nature's aborted has a nose that he dares to call his own and bite off at his own sweet will. Unfortunately, with an unthinkable fatuity we permit him to be told that but for the very agencies that have put him in possession he could successfully assert a God-given and world-old right to the noses of others. At present the honest fellow is mainly engaged in refreshing himself upon his own nose, consuming that comestible with avidity and precision; but the Vaillants, Ravechols, Mosts and Willeys are pointing his appetite to other snouts than his, and inspiring him with rhinophagic ambition. Meantime the rest of us are using those imperiled organs to snore with.

'Tis a fine, resonant and melodious snore, but it is not going to last: there is to be a rude awakening. We shall one day get our eyes open to the fact that scoundrels like Vaillant are neither few nor distant. We shall learn that our blind dependence upon the magic of words is a fatuous error; that the fortuitous arrangement of consonants and vowels which we worship as Liberty is of slight efficacy in disarming the lunatic brandishing a bomb. Liberty, indeed! The murderous wretch loves it a deal better than we, and wants more of it. Liberty! one almost sickens of the word, so quick and glib it is on every lip--so destitute of meaning.

There is no such thing as abstract liberty; it is not even thinkable. If you ask me, "Do you favor liberty?" I reply, "Liberty for whom to do what? Just now I distinctly favor the liberty of the law to cut off the noses of anarchists caught red-handed or red-tongued. If they go in for mutilation let them feel what it is like. If they are not satisfied with the way that things have been going on since the wife of Duke Albert the Pious was held under water with a pole, and since the servitors of the Suabian nobleman cherished their vestigial ears, it is to be presumed that they favor reversion to that happy state. There is grave objection, but if we must we will. Let us begin (with moderation) by reverting **them**."

I favor mutilation for anarchists convicted of killing or inciting to kill--mutilation followed by death. For those who merely deny the right and expediency of law, plain mutilation--which might advantageously take the form of removal of the tongue.

Why not? Where is the injustice? Surely he who denies men's right to make laws will not invoke the laws that they have wickedly made! That were to say that they must not protect themselves, yet are bound to protect him. What! if I beat him will he call the useless and mischievous constabulary? If I draw out his tongue shall he (in the sign-language) demand it back, and failing of restitution (for surely I should cut it clean away) shall he have the law on me--the naughty law, instrument of the oppressor? Why? that "goes neare to be fonny!"

Two human beings can not live together in peace without laws--laws innumerable. Everything that either, in consideration of the other's wish or welfare, abstains from is inhibited by law, tacit or expressed. If there were in all the world none but they--if neither had come with any sense of obligation toward the other, both clean from creation, with nothing but brains to direct their conduct--every hour would evolve an understanding, that is to say, a law; every act would suggest one. They would have to agree not to kill nor harm each other. They must arrange their work and all their activities to secure the best advantage. These arrangements, agreements, understandings--what are they but laws? To live without law is to live alone. Every family is a miniature State with a complicate system of laws, a supreme authority and subordinate authorities down to the latest babe. And as he who is loudest in demanding liberty for himself is sternest in denying it to others, you may confidently go to the Maison Vaillant, or the Mosthaus, for a flawless example of the iron hand.

Laws of the State are as faulty and as faultily administered as those of the Family. Most of them have to be speedily and repeatedly "amended," many repealed, and of those permitted to stand, the greater number fall into disuse and are forgotten. Those who have to be entrusted with the duty of administering them have all the limitations of intelligence and defects of character by which the rest of us also are distinguished from the angels. In the wise governor, the just judge, the honest sheriff or the patient constable we have as rare a phenomenon as the faultless father. The good God has not given us a special kind of men upon whom to devolve the duty of seeing to the observance of the understandings that we call laws. Like all else that men do, this work is badly done. The best that we can hope for through all the failures, the injustice, the disheartening damage to individual rights and interests, is a fairly good general result, enabling us to walk abroad among our fellows unafraid, to meet even the tribesmen from another valley without too imminent peril of braining and evisceration. Of that small security the Anarchist would deprive us. But without that nothing is of value and we shall be willing to renounce all. Let us begin by depriving ourselves of the Anarchist.

Our system of civilization being the natural outgrowth of our wretched moral and intellectual natures, is open to criticism and subject to revision. Our laws, being of human origin, are faulty and their application is disappointing. Dissent, dissatisfaction, deprecation, proposals for a better system fortified with better laws more intelligently administered--these are permissible and should be welcome. The Socialist (when he is not carried away by zeal to pool issues with the Anarchist) has that in him which it does us good to hear. He may be wrong b all else, yet right in showing us wherein we ourselves are wrong. Anyhow, his mission is amendment, and so long as his paths are peace he has the right to walk therein, exhorting as he goes. The French Communist who does not preach Petroleum and It rectified is to be regarded with more than amusement, more than compassion. There is room for him and his fad; there are hospitable ears for his boast that Jesus Christ would have been a Communist if there had been Communes. They really did not "know everything down in Judee." But for the Anarchist, whose aim is not amendment, but destruction--not welfare to the race, but mischief to a part of it--not happiness for the future, but revenge for the past--for that animal there should be no close season, for that savage, no reservation. Society has not the right to grant life to one who denies the right to live. The protagonist of reversion to the regime of lacking noses should lack a nose.

It is difficult to say if the bomb-thrower, actual or potential, is greater as scoundrel or fool. Suppose his aim is to compel concession by terror. Can not the brute observe at each of his exploits a tightening of "the reins of power?" Through the necessity of guarding against him the mildest governments are becoming despotic, the most despotic more despotic. Does he suppose that "the rulers of the earth" are silly enough to make concessions that will not insure their safety? Can *he* give them security?

III.

Of all the wild asses that roam the plain, the wildest wild ass that roams the plain is indubitably the one that lifts his voice and heel against that socialism known as "public ownership of public utilities," on the ground of "principle." There may be honest, and in some degree intelligent, opposition on the ground of expediency. Many persons whom it is a pleasure to respect believe that a Government railway, for example, would be less efficiently managed than the same railway in private hands, and that political dangers lurk in the proposal so enormously to increase the number of Federal employes as Government ownership of railways would entail. They think, in other words, that the policy is inexpedient. It is a duty to reason with them, which, as a rule, one can do without being insulted. But the chap who greets the proposal with a howl of derision as "Socialism!" is not a respectable opponent. Eyes he has, but he sees not; ears--oh! very abundant ears--but he hears not the still, small voice of history nor the still smaller voice of common sense.

Obviously to those who, having eyes, do see, public ownership of anything is a step in the direction of Socialism, for perfect Socialism means public ownership of everything. But "principle" has nothing to do with it The principle of public ownership is already accepted and established. It has no visible opponents except in the camp of the Anarchists, and fewer of them are visible there than soap and water would reveal. Antagonists of the ***principle*** of Socialism lost their fight when the first human government held the dedicatory exercises of a Cave of Legislation. Since then the only question about the matter has been how far the ***extension*** of Socialism is expedient Some would draw the limiting line at one place, some at another; but only a fool thinks there can be government without it, or good government without a great deal of it (The fact that we have always had a great deal of it yet never had good government affirms nothing that it is worth while to consider.)

The word-worn example of our Postal Department is only one of a thousand instances of pure Socialism. If it did not exist how bitter an opposition a proposal to establish it would evoke from Adversaries of the Red Rag! The Government builds and operates bridges with general assent; but as the late General Walker pointed out, it might under some circumstances be more economical, or better otherwise, to build and operate a ferry boat, which is a floating bridge. But that would be opposed as rank Socialism.

The truth is that the men and women of principle are a pretty dangerous class, generally speaking--and they are generally speaking. It is they that hamper us in every war. It is they who, preventing concentration and regulation of un-abolishable evils, promote their distribution and liberty. Moral principles are pretty good things--for the young and those not well grounded in goodness. If one have an impediment in his thought, or is otherwise unequal to emergencies as they arise, it is safest to be provided beforehand with something to refer to in order that a right decision may be made without taking thought. But "spirits of a purer fire" prefer to decide each question as it comes up, and to act upon the merits of the case, unbound and unpledged. With a quick intelligence, a capable conscience and a habit of doing right automatically one has little need to burden one's mind and memory with a set of solemn principles formulated by owlish philosophers who do not happen to know that what is right is merely what, in the long run and with regard to the greater number of cases, is expedient Principle is not always an infallible guide. For illustration, it is not always expedient--that is, for the good of all concerned--to tell the truth, to be entirely just or merciful, to pay a debt. I can conceive a case in which it would be right to assassinate one's neighbor. Suppose him to be a desperate scoundrel of a chemist who has devised a means of setting the atmosphere afire. The man who should go through life on an inflexible line of principle would border his path with a havoc of human happiness.

What one may think perfect one may not always think desirable. By "perfect" one may mean merely complete, and the word was so used in my reference to Socialism. I am not myself an advocate of "perfect Socialism," but as to Government ownership of railways, there is doubtless a good deal to be said on both sides. One argument in its favor appears decisive; under a system subject to popular control the law of gravitation would be shorn of its preeminence as a means of removing personal property from the baggage car, and so far as it is applicable to that work might even be repealed.

IV.

When M. Casimir-Perier resigned the French Presidency there were those who regarded the act as weak, cowardly, undutiful and otherwise censurable. It seems to me the act, not of a feeble man, but of a strong one--not that of a coward, but that of a gentleman. Indeed, I hardly know where to look in history for an act more entirely gratifying to my sense of "the fitness of things" than this dignified notification to mankind that in consenting to serve one's country one does not relinquish the right to decent treatment--to immunity from factious opposition and abuse--to at least as much civil consideration as is due from the Church to the Devil.

M. Casimir-Perier did not seek the Presidency of the French Republic; it was thrust upon him against his protestations by an apparently almost unanimous mandate of the French people in an emergency which it was thought that he was the best man to meet. That he met it with modesty and courage was testified without dissent. That he afterward did anything to forfeit the confidence and respect that he then inspired is not true, and nobody believes it true. Yet in his letter of resignation he said, and said truly:

"For the last six months a campaign of slander and insult has been going on against the army, magistrates. Parliament and hierarchical Chief of State, and this license to disseminate social hatred continues to be called 'the liberty of thought.'"

And with a dignity to which it seems strange that any one could be insensible, he added:

"The respect and ambition which I entertain for my country will not allow me to acknowledge that the servants of the country, and he who represents it in the presence of foreign nations, may be insulted every day."

These are noble words. Have we any warrant for demanding or expecting that men of clean life and character will devote themselves to the good of ingrates who pay, and ingrates who permit them to pay, in flung mud? It is hardly credible that among even those persons most infatuated by contemplation of their own merit as pointed out by their thrifty sycophants "the liberty of thought" has been carried to that extreme. The right of the State to demand the sacrifice of the citizen's life is a doctrine as old as the patriotism that concedes it, but the right to require him to forego his good name--that is something new under the sun. From nothing but the dunghill of modern democracy could so noxious a plant have sprung.

"Perhaps in laying down my functions," said M. Casimir-Perier, "I shall have marked out a path of duty to those who are solicitous for the dignity, power and good name of France in the world."

We may be permitted to hope that the lesson is wider than France and more lasting than the French Republic. It is time that not only France but all other countries with "popular institutions" should learn that if they wish to command the services of men of honor they must accord them honorable treatment; the rule now is for the party to which they belong to give them a half-hearted support while suffering all other parties to slander and insult them. The action of the President of the French Republic in these disgusting circumstances is exceptional and unusual only in respect of his courage in expressly resenting his wrong. Everywhere the unreasonable complaint is heard that good men will not "go into politics;" everywhere the ignorant and malignant masses and their no less malignant and hardly less ignorant leaders and spokesmen, having sown the wind of reasonless obstruction and partisan vilification, are reaping the whirlwind of misrule. So far as concerns the public service, gentlemen are mostly on a strike against introduction of the mud-machine. This high-minded political workman, Casimir-Perier, never showed to so noble advantage as in gathering up his tools and walking out.

It may be, and a million times has been, urged that abstention from activity in public affairs by men of brains and character leaves the business of government in the hands of the incapable and the vicious. In whose hands, pray, in a republic does it logically belong? What does the theory of "representative government" affirm? What is the lesson of every netherward extension of the suffrage? What do we mean by permitting it to "broaden slowly down" to lower and lower intelligences and moralities?--what but that stupidity and vice, equally with virtue and wisdom, are entitled to a voice in political affairs, a finger in the public pie?

A person that is fit to vote is fit to be voted for. He who is competent for the high and difficult function of choosing an officer of the State is competent to serve the State as an officer. To deny him the right is illogical and unjust. Participation in Government can not be at the same time a privilege and a duty, and he who claims it as a privilege must not speak of another's renunciation (whereby himself is more highly privileged) as "shirking." With every retirement from politics increased power passes to those who remain. Shall they protest? Shall they, also, who have retired? Who else is to protest? The complaint of "incivism" would be more rational if there were some one by whom it could reasonably be made.

My advice to slandered officials has ever been: "Resign." The public officials of this favored country, Heaven be thanked, are infrequently slandered: they are, as a rule, so bad that calumniation is a compliment. Our best men, with here and there an exception, have been driven out of public life, or made afraid to enter it. Even our spasmodic efforts at reform fail ludicrously for lack of leaders unaffiliated with "the thing to be reformed." Unless attracted by the salary, why should a gentleman "aspire" to the Presidency of the United States? During his canvass (and he is expected to "run," not merely to "stand") he will have from his own party a support that should make him blush, and from all the others an opposition that will stick at nothing to accomplish his satisfactory defamation. After his election his partition and allotment of the loaves and fishes will estrange an important and thenceforth implacable faction of his following without appeasing the animosity of any one else; and during his entire service his sky will be dark with a flight of dead cats. At the finish of his term the utmost that he can expect in the way of reward not expressible in terms of the national currency is that not much more than one-half of his countrymen will believe him a scoundrel to the end of their days.

V.

The kind of government that we have seems to me one of the worst kinds extant A government that does not protect life is a flat failure, no matter what else it may do. Life being almost universally regarded as the most precious possession, its security is the first and highest essential--not the life of him who takes life, but the life which is exposed defenceless to his hateful hand. In no country in the world, civilized or savage, is life so insecure as in this. In no country in the world is murder held in so light reprobation. In no battle of modern times have so many lives been taken as are lost annually in the United States through public indifference to the crime of homicide--through disregard of law, through bad government. If American self-government, with its ten thousand homicides a year, is good government, there is no such thing as bad. Self-government! What monstrous nonsense! Who governs himself needs no government, has no governor, is not governed. If government has any meaning it means the restraint of the many by the few--the subordination of numbers to brains. It means the determined denial to the masses of the right to cut their own throats. It means the grasp and control of all the social forces and material enginery--a vigilant censorship of the press, a firm hand upon the church, keen supervision of public meetings and public amusements, command of the railroads, telegraph and all means of communication. It means, in short, the ability to make use of all the beneficent influences of enlightenment for the good of the people, and to array all the powers of civilization against civilization's natural enemies--the people. Government like this has a thousand defects, but it has one merit: it is government.

Despotism? Yes. It is the despotisms of the world that have been the conservators of civilization. It is the despot who, most powerful for mischief, is alone powerful for good. It is conceded that government is necessary--even by the "fierce democracies" that madly renounce it. But in so far as government is not despotic it is not government. In Europe for the last one hundred years, the tendency of all government has been liberalization. The history of European politics during that period is a history of renunciation by the rulers and assumption by the ruled. Sovereign after sovereign has surrendered prerogative after prerogative; the nobility privilege after privilege. Mark the result: society honeycombed with treason; property menaced with partition; assassination studied as a science and practiced as an art; everywhere powerful secret organizations sworn to demolish the social fabric that the slow centuries have but just erected and unmindful that themselves will perish in the wreck. No heart in Europe can beat tranquilly under clean linen. Such is the gratitude, such is the wisdom, such the virtue of "The Masses." In 1863 Alexander II of Russia freed 25,000,000 serfs. In 1879 they had killed him and all joined the conspirators.

That ancient and various device, "a republican form of government," appears to be too good for all the peoples of the earth excepting one. It is partly successful in Switzerland; in France and America, where the majority is composed of persons having dark understandings and criminal instincts, it has broken down. In our case, as in every case, the momentum of successful revolution carried us too far. We rebelled against tyranny and having overthrown it, overthrew also the governmental form in which it had happened to be manifest. In their anger and their triumph our good old gran'thers acted somewhat in the spirit of the Irishman who cudgeled the dead snake until nothing was left of it, in order to make it "sinsible of its desthroction." They meant it all, too, the honest souls! For a long time after the setting up of the republic the republic meant active hatred to kings, nobles, aristocracies. It was held, and rightly held, that a nobleman could not breathe in America--that he left his title and his privileges on the ship that brought him over. Do we observe anything of that in this generation? On the landing of a foreign king, prince or nobleman--even a miserable "knight"--do we not execute sycophantic genuflexions? Are not our newspapers full of flamboyant descriptions and qualming adulation? Nay, does not our President himself--successor to Washington and Jefferson!--greet and entertain the "nation's guest"? Is not every American young woman crazy to mate with a male of title? Does all this represent no retrogression?--is it not the backward movement of the shadow on the dial? Doubtless the republican idea has struck strong roots into the soil of the two Americas, but he who rightly considers the tendencies of events, the causes that bring them about and the consequences that flow from them, will not be hot to affirm the perpetuity of republican institutions in the Western Hemisphere. Between their inception and their present stage of development there is scarcely the beat of a pendulum; and already, by corruption and lawlessness, the people of both continents, with all their diversities of race and character, have shown themselves about equally unfit. To become a nation of scoundrels all that any people needs is opportunity, and what we are pleased to call by the impossible name of "self-government" supplies it.

The capital defect of republican government is inability to repress internal forces tending to disintegration. It does not take long for a "self-governed" people to learn that it is not really governed--that an agreement enforcible by nobody but the parties to it is not binding. We are learning this very rapidly: we set aside our laws whenever we please. The sovereign power--the tribunal of ultimate jurisdiction--

is a mob. If the mob is large enough (it need not be very large), even if composed of vicious tramps, it may do as it will. It may destroy property and life. It may without proof of guilt inflict upon individuals torments unthinkable by fire and flaying, mutilations that are nameless. It may call men, women and children from their beds and beat them to death with cudgels. In the light of day it may assail the very strongholds of law in the heart of a populous city, and assassinate prisoners of whose guilt it knows nothing. And these things--observe, O victims of kings--are habitually done. One would as well be at the mercy of one's sovereign as of one's neighbor.

For generations we have been charming ourselves with the magic of words. When menaced by some exceptionally monstrous form of the tyranny of numbers we have closed our eyes and murmured, "Liberty." When armed Anarchists threaten to quench the fires of civilization in a sea of blood we prate of the protective power of "free speech." If,

"Girt about by friends or foes,
A man may speak the thing he will,"

we fondly fancy that the thing he will speak is harmless--that immunity disarms his tongue of its poison, his thought of its infection. With a fatuity that would be incredible without the testimony of observation, we hold that an Anarchist free to go about making proselytes, free to purchase arms, free to drill and parade and encourage his dupes with a demonstration of their numbers and power, is less mischievous than an Anarchist with a shut mouth, a weaponless hand and under surveillance of the police. The Anarchist himself is persuaded of the superiority of our plan of dealing with him; he likes it and comes over in quantity, inpesting the political atmosphere with the "sweltered venom" engendered by centuries of oppression--comes over here, where he is not oppressed, and sets up as oppressor. His preferred field of malefaction is the country that is most nearly anarchical. He comes here, partly to better himself under our milder institutions, partly to secure immunity while conspiring to destroy them. There is thunder in Europe, but if the storm ever break it is in America that the lightning will fall, for here is a great vortex into which the decivilizing agencies are pouring without obstruction. Here gather the eagles to the feast, for the quarry is defenceless. Here is no power in government, no government. Here an enemy of order is thought to be least dangerous when suffered to preach and arm in peace. And here is nothing between him and his task of supervision--no pampered soldiery to repress his rising, no iron authority to lay him by the heels. The militia is fraternal, the magistracy elective. Europe may hold out a little longer. The Great Powers may make what stage-play they will, but they are not maintaining their incalculable armaments for aggression upon one another, for protection from one another, nor for fun. These vast forces are purely constabular--creatures and creators of discontent--phenomena of decivilization. Eventually they will fraternize with Disorder or become themselves Praetorian Guards more dangerous than the perils that have called them into existence.

It is easy to forecast the first stages of the End's approach: Rioting. Disaffection of constabulary and troops. Subversion of the Government A policy of decapitation. Upthrust of the serviceable Anarchist. His prompt effacement by his victorious ally and natural enemy, the Socialist. Free minting and printing of money--to every citizen a shoulder-load of the latter, to the printers a ton each. Divided counsels. Pandemonium. The man on horseback. Gusts of grape. ------?

Formerly the bearer of evil tidings was only slain; he is now ignored. The gods kept their secrets by telling them to Cassandra, whom no one would believe. I do not expect to be heeded. The crust of a volcano is electric the fumes are narcotic; the combined sensation is delightful no end. I have looked at the dial of civilization; I tell you the shadow is going back. That is of small importance to men of leisure, with wine-dipped wreaths upon their heads. They do not care to know.

CIVILIZATION

I.

THE question "Does civilization civilize?" is a fine example of **petitio principii**. and decides itself in the affirmative; for civilization must needs do that from the doing of which it has its name. But it is not necessary to suppose that he who propounds is either unconscious of his lapse in logic or desirous of digging a pitfall for the feet of those who discuss; I take it he simply wishes to put the matter in an impressive way, and relies upon a certain degree of intelligence in the interpretation.

Concerning uncivilized peoples we know but little except what we are told by travelers--who, speaking generally, can know very little but the fact of uncivilization as shown in externals and irrelevances, and are moreover, greatly given to lying. From the savages we hear very little. Judging them in all things by our own standards, in default of a knowledge of theirs, we necessarily condemn, disparage and belittle. One thing that civilization certainly has not done is to make us intelligent enough to understand that the opposite of a virtue is not necessarily a vice. Because we do not like the taste of one another it does not follow that the cannibal is a person of depraved appetite. Because, as a rule, we have but one wife and several mistresses each it is not certain that polygamy is everywhere--nor, for that matter, anywhere--either wrong or inexpedient. Our habit of wearing clothes does not prove that conscience of the body, the sense of shame, is charged with a divine mandate; for like the conscience of the spirit it is the creature of what it seems to create: it comes to the habit of wearing clothes. And for those who hold that the purpose of civilization is morality it may be said that peoples which are the most nearly naked are, in our sense, the most nearly moral. Because the brutality of the civilized slave owners and dealers created a conquering sentiment against slavery it is not intelligent to assume that slavery is a maleficent thing amongst Oriental peoples (for example) where the slave is not oppressed.

Some of these same Orientals whom we are pleased to term half-civilized have no regard for truth. "Takest thou me for a Christian dog," said one of them, "that I should be the slave of my word?" So far as I can perceive the "Christian dog" is no more the slave of his word than the True Believer, and I think the savage--allowing for the fact that his inveracity has dominion over fewer things--as great a liar as either of them. For my part, I do not know what, in all circumstances, is right or wrong; but I know, if right, it is at least stupid to judge an uncivilized people by the standards of morality and intelligence set up by civilized ones. An infinitesimal proportion of civilized men do not, and there is much to be said for civilization if they are the product of it.

Life in civilized countries is so complex that men there have more ways to be good than savages have, and more to be bad; more to be happy, and more to be miserable. And in each way to be good or bad, their generally superior knowledge--

their knowledge of more things--enables them to commit greater excesses than the savage could widi the same opportunity. The civilized philanthropist wreaks upon his fellow creatures a ranker philanthropy, the civilized scoundrel a sturdier rascality. And--splendid triumph of enlightenment!--the two characters are, in civilisation, commonly combined in one person.

I know of no savage custom or habit of thought which has not its mate in civilized countries. For every mischievous or absurd practice of the natural man I can name you a dozen of the unnatural which are essentially the same. And nearly every custom of our barbarian ancestors in historic times survives in some form today. We make ourselves look formidable in battle--for that matter, we fight. Our women paint their faces. We feel it obligatory to dress more or less alike, inventing the most ingenious reasons for it and actually despising and persecuting those who do not care to conform. Within the memory of living persons bearded men were stoned in the streets; and a clergyman in New York who wore his beard as Christ wore his, was put into jail and variously persecuted till he died. We bury our dead instead of burning them, yet every cemetery is set thick with urns. As there are no ashes for the urns we do not trouble ourselves to make them hollow, and we say their use is "emblematic." When, following the bent of our ancestral instincts, we go on, age after age, in the performance of some senseless act which once had a use and meaning we excuse ourselves by calling it symbolism. Our "symbols" are merely survivals. We have theology and patriotism. We have all the savage's superstition. We propitiate and ingratiate by means of gifts. We shake hands. All these and hundreds of others of our practices are distinctly, in their nature and by their origin, savage.

Civilization does not, I think, make the race any better. It makes men know more: and if knowledge makes them happy it is useful and desirable. The one purpose of every sane human being is to be happy. No one can have any other motive than that. There is no such thing as unselfishness. We perform the most "generous" and "self-sacrificing" acts because we should be unhappy if we did not. We move on lines of least reluctance. Whatever tends to increase the beggarly sum of human happiness is worth having; nothing else has any value.

The cant of civilization fatigues. Civilization is a fine and beautiful structure. It is as picturesque as a Gothic cathedral. But it is built upon the bones and cemented with the blood of those whose part in all its pomp is that and nothing more. It cannot be reared in the generous tropics, for there the people will not contribute their blood and bones. The proposition that the average American workingman or European peasant is "better off" than the South Sea Islander, lolling under a palm and drunk with over-eating, will not bear a moment's examination.

It is we scholars and gentlemen that are better off.

It is admitted that the South Sea Islander in a state of nature is overmuch addicted to the practice of eating human flesh; but concerning that I submit: first, that he likes it; second, that those who supply it are mostly dead. It is upon his enemies that he feeds, and these he would kill anyhow, as we do ours. In civilized, enlightened and Christian countries, where cannibalism has not yet established itself, wars are as frequent and destructive as among the maneaters. The untitled savage knows at least why he goes killing, whereas the private soldier is commonly in black ignorance of the apparent cause of quarrel--of the actual cause, always. Their shares in the fruits of victory are about equal: the Chief takes all the dead, the General all the glory. Moreover it costs more human life to supply a Christian gentleman with food than it does a cannibal--with food alone: "board;" if you could figure out the number of lives that his lodging, clothing, amusements and accomplishment cost the sum would startle. Happily *he* does not pay it. Considering human lives as having value, cannibalism is undoubtedly the more economical system.

II.

Transplanted institutions grow but slowly; and civilization can not be put into a ship and carried across an ocean. The history of this country is a sequence of illustrations of these truths. It was settled by civilized men and women from civilized countries, yet after two and a half centuries with unbroken communication with the mother systems, it is still imperfectly civilized. In learning and letters, in art and the science of government, America is but a faint and stammering echo of England.

For nearly all that is good in our American civilization we are indebted to England; the errors and mischiefs are of our own creation. We have originated little, because there is little to originate, but we have unconsciously reproduced many of the discredited and abandoned systems of former ages and other countries--receiving them at second hand, but making them ours by the sheer strength and immobility of the national belief in their newness. Newness! Why, it is not possible to make an experiment in government, in art, in literature, in sociology, or in morals, that has not been made over, and over, and over again. Fools talk of clear and simple remedies for this and that evil afflicting the commonwealth. If a proposed remedy is obvious and easily intelligible, it is condemned in the naming, for it is morally certain to have been tried a thousand times in the history of the world, and had it been effective men ere now would have forgotten, from mere disuse, how to produce the evil it cured.

There are clear and simple remedies for nothing. In medicine there has been discovered but a single specific; in politics not one. The interests, moral and natural, of a community in our highly differentiated civilization are so complex, intricate, delicate and interdependent, that you can not touch one without affecting all. It is a familiar truth that no law was ever passed that did not have unforeseen results; but of these results, by far the greater number are never recognized as of its creation. The best that can be said of any "measure" is, that the sum of its perceptible benefits seems so to exceed the sum of its perceptible evils as to constitute a balance of advantage. Yet the magnificent innocence of the statesman or philosopher to whose understanding "the whole matter lies in a nutshell"--who thinks he can formulate a practical political or social policy within the four corners of an epigram--who fears nothing because he knows nothing--is constantly to the fore with a simple specific for ills whose causes are complex, constant and inscrutable. To the understanding of this creature a difficulty well ignored is half overcome; so he buttons up his eyes and assails the problems of life with the divine confidence of a blind pig traversing a labyrinth.

The glories of England are our glories. She can achieve nothing that our fathers did not help to make possible to her. The learning, the power, the refinement of a great nation, are not the growth of a century, but of many centuries; each generation builds upon the work of the preceding. For untold ages our ancestors wrought to rear that "revered pile," the civilization of England. And shall we now try to belittle the mighty structure because other though kindred hands are laying the top courses while we have elected to found a new tower in another land? The American eulogist of civilization who is not proud of his heritage in England's glory is unworthy to enjoy his lesser heritage in the lesser glory of his own country.

The English are undoubtedly our intellectual superiors; and as the virtues are solely the product of education--a rogue being only a dunce considered from another point of view--they are our moral superiors likewise. Why should they not be? It is a land not of log and pine-board schoolhouses grudgingly erected and containing schools supported by such niggardly tax levies as a sparse and hard-handed population will consent to pay, but of ancient institutions splendidly endowed by the State and by centuries of private benefaction. As a means of dispensing formulated ignorance our boasted public school system is not without merit; it spreads it out sufficiently thin to give everyone enough to make him a more competent fool than he would have been without it; but to compare it with that which is not the creature of legislation acting with malice aforethought, but the unnoted outgrowth of ages, is to be ridiculous. It is like comparing the laid-out town of a western prairie, its right-angled streets, prim cottages, "built on the installment plan," and its wooden a-b-c shops, with the grand old town of Oxford, topped with the clustered domes and towers of its twenty-odd great colleges; the very names of many of whose founders have perished from human record as have all the chronicles of the times in which they lived.

It is not alone that we have had to "subdue the wilderness;" our educational conditions are otherwise adverse. Our political system is unfavorable. Our fortunes, accumulated in one generation, are dispersed in the next. If it takes three generations to make a gentleman one will not make a thinker. Instruction is acquired, but capacity for instruction is transmitted. The brain that is to contain a trained intellect is not the result of a haphazard marriage between a clown and a wench, nor does it get its tractable tissues from a hard-headed farmer and a soft-headed milliner. If you confess the importance of race and pedigree in a race horse and a bird dog how dare you deny it in a man?

I do not claim that the political and social system that creates an aristocracy of leisure, and consequently of intellect, is the best possible kind of human organization; I perceive its disadvantages clearly enough. But I do not hold that a system under which all important public trusts, political and professional, civil and military, ecclesiastical and secular, are held by educated men--that is, men of trained faculties and disciplined judgment--is not an altogether faulty system.

It is only in our own country that an exacting literary taste is believed to disqualify a man for purveying to the literary needs of a taste less exacting--a proposition obviously absurd, for an exacting taste is nothing but the intelligent discrimination of a judgment instructed by comparison and observation. There is, in fact, no pursuit or occupation, from that of a man who blows up a balloon to that of the man who bores out the stove pipes, in which he that has talent and education is not a better worker than he that has either, and he than he that has neither. It is a universal human weakness to disparage the knowledge that we do not ourselves possess, but it is only my own beloved country that can justly boast herself the last refuge and asylum of the impotents and incapables who deny the advantage of all knowledge whatsoever. It was an American Senator (Logan) who declared that he had devoted a couple of weeks to the study of finance, and found the accepted authorities all wrong. It was another American Senator (Morton) who, confronted with certain ugly facts in the history of another country, proposed "to brush away all facts, and argue the question on considerations of plain common sense."

Republican institutions have this disadvantage: by incessant changes in the ***personnel*** of government--to say nothing of the manner of men that ignorant constituencies elect; and all constituencies are ignorant--we attain to no fixed principles and standards. There is no such thing here as a science of politics, because it is not to any one's interest to make politics the study of his life. Nothing is settled; no truth finds general acceptance. What we do one year we undo the next, and do over again the year following. Our energy is wasted in, and our prosperity suffers from, experiments endlessly repeated.

One of the disadvantages of our social system, which is the child of our political, is the tyranny of public opinion, forbidding the utterance of wholesome but unpalatable truth. In a republic we are so accustomed to the rule of majorities that it seldom occurs to us to examine their title to dominion; and as the ideas of might and right are, by our innate sense of justice, linked together, we come to consider public opinion infallible and almost sacred. Now, majorities rule, not because they are right, but because they are able to rule. In event of collision they would conquer, so it is expedient for minorities to submit beforehand to save trouble. In fact, majorities, embracing, as they do the most ignorant, seldom think rightly; public opinion, being the opinion of mediocrity, is commonly a mistake and a mischief. But it is to nobody's interest--it is against the interest of most--to dispute with it. Public writer and public speaker alike find their account in confirming "the plain people" in their brainless errors and brutish prejudices--in glutting their omnivorous vanity and inflaming their implacable racial and national hatreds.

I have long held the opinion that patriotism is one of the most abominable vices affecting the human understanding. Every patriot in this world believes his country better than any other country. Now, they cannot all be the best; indeed, only one can be the best, and it follows that the patriots of all the others have suffered themselves to be misled by a mere sentiment into blind unreason. In its active manifestation--it is fond of shooting--patriotism would be well enough if it were simply defensive; but it is also aggressive, and the same feeling that prompts us to strike for our altars and our fires impels us likewise to go over the border to quench the fires and overturn the altars of our neighbors. It is all very pretty and spirited, what the poets tell us about Thermopylae, but there was as much patriotism at one end of that pass as there was at the other. Patriotism deliberately and with folly aforethought subordinates the interests of a whole to the interests of a part. Worse still, the fraction so favored is determined by an accident of birth or residence. Patriotism is like a dog which, having entered at random one of a row of kennels, suffers more in combats with the dogs in the other kennels than it would have done by sleeping in the open air. The hoodlum who cuts the tail from a Chinamen's nowl, and would cut the nowl from the body if he dared, is simply a patriot with a logical mind, having the courage of his opinions. Patriotism is fierce as a fever, pitiless as the grave, blind as a stone and irrational as a headless hen.

There are two ways of clarifying liquids--ebullition and precipitation; one forces the impurities to the surface as scum, the other sends them to the bottom as dregs. The former is the more offensive, and that seems to be our way; but neither is useful if the impurities are merely separated but not removed. We are told with tiresome iteration that our social and political systems are clarifying; but when is the skimmer to appear? If the purpose of free institutions is good government where is the good government?--when may it be expected to begin?--how is it to come about? Systems of government have no sanctity; they are practical means to a simple end--the public welfare; worthy of no respect if they fail of its accomplishment. The tree is known by its fruit. Ours, is bearing crab-apples.

If the body politic is constitutionally diseased, as I verily believe; if the disorder inheres in the system; there is no remedy. The fever must burn itself out, and then Nature will do the rest. One does not prescribe what time alone can administer. We have put our criminal class in power; do we suppose they will efface themselves? Will they restore to *us* the power of governing *them*? They must have their way and go their length. The natural and immemorial sequence is: tyranny, insurrection, combat. In combat everything that wears a sword has a chance--even the right. History does not forbid us to hope. But it forbids us to rely upon numbers; they will be against us. If history teaches anything worth learning it teaches that the majority of mankind is neither good nor wise. Where government is founded upon the public conscience and the public intelligence the stability of States is a dream. Nor have we any warrant for the Tennysonian faith that

> "Freedom broadens slowly down
> From precedent to precedent."

In that moment of time that is covered by historical records we have abundant evidence that each generation has believed itself wiser and better than any of its predecessors; that each people has believed itself to have the secret of national perpetuity. In support of this universal delusion there is nothing to be said; the desolate places of the earth cry out against it. Vestiges of obliterated civilizations cover the earth; no savage but has camped upon the sites of proud and populous cities; no desert but has heard the statesman's boast of national stability. Our nation, our laws, our history--all shall go down to everlasting oblivion with the others, and by the same road. But I submit that we are traveling it with needless haste.

But it is all right and righteous. It can be spared--this Jonah's gourd civilization of ours. We have hardly the rudiments of a true civilization; compared with the splendors of which we catch dim glimpses in the fading past, ours are as an illumination of tallow candles. We know no more than the ancients; we only know other things, but nothing in which is an assurance of perpetuity, and little that is truly wisdom. Our vaunted *elixir vito* is the art of printing with moveable types. What good will those do when posterity, struck by the inevitable intellectual blight, shall have ceased to read what is printed? Our libraries will become its stables, our books its fuel.

Ours is a civilization that might be heard from afar in space as a scolding and a riot; a civilization in which the race has so differentiated as to have no longer a community of interest and feeling; which shows as a ripe result of the principles underlying it a reasonless and rascally feud between rich and poor; in which one is offered a choice (if one have the means to take it) between American plutocracy and European militocracy, with an imminent chance of renouncing either for a stultocratic republic with a headsman in the presidential chair and every laundress in exile.

I have not a "solution" to the "labor problem." I have only a story. Many and many years ago lived a man who was so good and wise that none in all the world was so good and wise as he. He was one of those few whose goodness and wisdom are such that after some time has passed their fellowmen begin to think them gods and treasure their words as divine law; and by millions they are worshiped through centuries of time. Amongst the utterances of this man was one command--not a new nor perfect one--which has seemed to his adorers so preeminently wise that they have given it a name by which it is known over half the world. One of the sovereign virtues of this famous law is its simplicity, which is such that all hearing must understand; and obedience is so easy that any nation refusing is unfit to exist except in the turbulence and adversity that will surely come to it. When a people would avert want and strife, or having them, would restore plenty and peace, this noble commandment offers the only means--all other plans for safety or relief are as vain as dreams, and as empty as the crooning of fools. And behold, here it is: "All things whatsoever ye would that men should do to you, do ye even so to them."

What! you unappeasable rich, coining the sweat and blood of your workmen into drachmas, understanding the law of supply and demand as mandatory and justifying your cruel greed by the senseless dictum that "business is business;" you lazy workman, railing at the capitalist by whose desertion, when you have frightened away his capital, you starve--rioting and shedding blood and torturing and poisoning by way of answer to exaction and by way of exaction; you foul anarchists, applauding with indelicate palms when one of your coward kind hurls a bomb amongst powerless and helpless women and children; you imbecile politicians with a plague of remedial legislation for the irremediable; you writers and thinkers un-read in history, with as many "solutions to the labor problem" as there are dunces among you who can not coherently define it--do you really think yourself wiser than Jesus of Nazareth? Do you seriously suppose yourselves competent to amend his plan for dealing with all the evils besetting states and souls? Have you the ef-frontery to believe that those who spurn his Golden Rule you can bind to obedience of an act entitled an act to amend an act? Bah! you fatigue the spirit. Go get ye to your scoundrel lockouts, your villain strikes, your blacklisting, your boycotting, your speech-ing, marching and maundering; but if ye do not to others as ye would that they do to you it shall occur, and that right soon, that ye be drowned in your own blood and your pickpocket civilization quenched as a star that falls into the sea.

THE GAME OF POLITICS
I.

IF ONE were to declare himself a Democrat or a Republican and the claim should be contested he would find it a difficult one to prove. The missing link in his chain of evidence would be the major premise in the syllogism necessary to the establishment of his political status--a definition of "Democrat" or "Republican." Most of the statesmen in public and private life who are poll-parroting these words, do so with entire unconsciousness of their meaning, or rather without knowledge that they have lost whatever of meaning they once had. The words are mere "sur-vivals," marking dead issues and covering allegiances of the loosest and most shal-low character. On any question of importance each party is divided against itself and dares not formulate a preference. There is no question before the country upon which one may not think and vote as he likes without affecting his standing in the political communion of saints of which he professes himself a member. "Party lines" are as terribly confused as the parallels of latitude and longitude after a twisting earthquake, or those aimless lines representing the competing railroad on a map published by a company operating "the only direct route." It is not probable that this state of things can last; if there is to be "government by party"--and we should be sad to think that so inestimable a boon were soon to return to Him who gave it--men must begin to let their angry passions rise and take rides. "Ill fares the land to hastening ills a prey," where the people are too wise to dispute and too good to fight. Let us have the good old political currency of bloody noses and cracked crowns; let the yawp of the demagogue be heard in the land; let ears be pestered with the spargent cheers of the masses. Give us a whoop-up that shall rouse us like a rattling peal of thunder. Will nobody be our Moses--there should be two Moseses--to lead us through this detestable wilderness of political stagnation?

II.

Nowhere "on God's green earth"--it is fitting, that this paper contain a bit of bosh--nowhere is so much insufferable stuff talked in a given period of time as in an American political convention. It is there that all those objectionable elements of the national character which evoke the laughter of Europe and are the despair of our friends find freest expression, unhampered by fear of any censorship more exacting than that of "the opposing party"--which takes no account of intellectual delinquencies, but only of moral. The "organs" of the "opposing party" will not take the trouble to point out--even to observe--that the "debasing sentiments" and "criminal views" uttered in speech and platform are expressed in sickening syntax and offensive rhetoric. Doubtless an American politician, statesman, what you will, could go into a political convention and signify his views with simple, unpretentious common sense, but doubtless he never does.

Every community is cursed with a number of "orators"--men regarded as "eloquent"--"silver tongued" men--fellows who to the common American knack at brandishing the tongue add an exceptional felicity of platitude, a captivating mastery of dog's-eared sentiment, a copious and obedient vocabulary of eulogium, an iron insensibility to the ridiculous and an infinite affinity to fools. These afflicting Chrysostoms are always lying in wait for an "occasion" It matters not what it is: a "reception" to some great man from abroad, a popular ceremony like the laying of a corner-stone, the opening of a fair, the dedication of a public building, an anniversary banquet of an ancient and honorable order (they all belong to ancient and honorable orders) or a club dinner--they all belong to clubs and pay dues. But it is in the political convention that they come out particularly strong. By some imperious tradition having the force of written law it is decreed that in these absurd bodies of our fellow citizens no word of sense shall be uttered from the platform; whatever is uttered in set speeches shall be addressed to the meanest capacity present As a chain can be no stronger than its weakest link, so nothing said by the speakers at a political convention must be above the intellectual reach of the most pernicious idiot having a seat and a vote. I don't know why it is so. It seems to be thought that if he is not suitably entertained he will not attend, as a delegate, the next convention.

Here are the opening sentences of the speech in which a man was once nominated for Governor:

"Two years ago the Republican party in State and Nation marched to imperial triumph. On every hilltop and mountain peak our beacons blazed and we awakened the echoes of every valley with songs of our rejoicings."

And so forth. Now, if I were asked to recast those sentences so that they should conform to the simple truth and be inoffensive to good taste I should say something like this:

"Two years ago the Republican party won a general election."

If there is any thing in this inflated rigmarole that is not adequately expressed in my amended statement, what is it? As to eloquence it will hardly be argued that nonsense, falsehood and metaphors which were old when Rome was young are essential to that. The first man (in early Greece) who spoke of awakening an echo did a felicitous thing. Was it felicitous in the second? Is it felicitous now? As to that military metaphor--the "marching" and so forth--its inventor was as great an ass as any one of the incalculable multitude of his plagiarists. On this matter hear the late Richard Grant White:

"Is it not time that we had done with the nauseous talk about campaigns, and standard-bearers, and glorious victories (imperial triumphs) and all the bloated army-bumming bombast which is so rife for the six months preceding an election? To read almost any one of our political papers during a canvass is enough to make one sick and sorry.... An election has no manner of likeness to a campaign, or a battle. It is not even a contest in which the stronger or more dexterous party is the winner; it is a mere counting, in which the bare fact that one party is the more numerous puts it in power if it will only come up and be counted; to insure which a certain time is spent by each party in reviling and belittling the candidates of its opponents and lauding its own; and this is the canvass, at the likening of which to a campaign every honest soldier might reasonably take offense."

But, after all, White was only "one o' them dam litery fellers," and I dare say the original proponent of the military metaphor, away off there in "the dark backward and abysm of time," knew a lot more about practical politics than White ever did. And it is practical politics to be an ass.

In withdrawing his own name from before a convention, a California politician once made a purely military speech of which a single sample passage is all that I shall allow myself the happiness to quote:

"I come before you today as a Republican of the Republican banner county of this great State of ours. From snowy Shasta on the north to sunny Diego on the south; from the west, where the waves of the Pacific look upon our shores, to where the barriers of the great Sierras stand clad in eternal snow, there is no more loyal county to the Republican party in this State than the county from which I hail. [Applause, naturally.] Its loyalty to the party has been tested on many fields of battle [Anglice, in many elections] and it has never wavered in the contest Wherever the fate of battle was trembling in the balance [Homer, and since Homer, Tom, Dick and Harry] Alameda county stepped into the breach and rescued the Republican party from defeat."

Translated into English this military mouthing would read somewhat like this:

"I live in Alameda county, where the Republicans have uniformly outvoted the Democrats."

The orators at the Democratic convention a week earlier were no better and no different. Their rhetorical stock-in-trade was the same old shop-worn figures of speech in which their predecessors have dealt for ages, and in which their successors will traffic to the end of--well, to the end of that imitative quality in the national character, which, by its superior intensity, serves to distinguish us from the apes that perish.

III.

"What we most need, to secure honest elections," says a well-meaning reform-er, "is the Clifford or the Myers voting machine." Why, truly, here is a hopeful spirit--a rare and radiant intelligence suffused with the conviction that men can be made honest by machinery--that human character is a matter of gearing, ratchets and dials! One would give something to know how it feels to be like that. A mind so constituted must be as happy in its hope as a hen incubating a nest-ful of porcelain door-knobs. It lives in rapturous contemplation of a world of its own creation--a world where public morality and political good order are to be had by purchase at the machine-shop. In that delectable world religion is superfluous; the true high priest is the mechanical engineer; the minor clergy are the village blacksmiths. It is rather a pity that so fine and fair a sphere should prosper only in the attenuated ether of an idiot's understanding.

Voting-machines are doubtless well enough; they save labor and enable the statesmen of the street to know the result within a few minutes of the closing of the polls--whereby many are spared to their country who would otherwise incur fatal disorders by exposure to the night air while assisting in awaiting the returns. But a voting-machine that human ingenuity can not pervert, human ingenuity can not invent.

That is true, too, of laws. Your statesman of a mental stature somewhat over-topping that of the machine-person puts his faith in law. Providence has designed to permit him to be persuaded of the efficacy of statutes--good, stringent, carefully drawn statutes definitively repealing all the laws of nature in conflict with any of their provisions. So the poor devil (I am writing of Mr. Legion) turns for relief from law to law, ever on the stool of repentance, yet ever unfouling the anchor of hope. By no power cm earth can his indurated understanding be penetrated by the truth that his woful state is due, not to any laws of his own, nor to any lack of them, but to his rascally refusal to obey the Golden Rule. How long is it since we were all clam-oring for the Australian ballot law, which was to make a new Heaven and a new earth? We have the Australian ballot law and the same old earth smelling to the same old Heaven. Writhe upon the triangle as we may, groan out what new laws we will, the pitiless thong will fall upon our bleeding backs as long as we deserve it. If our sins, which are scarlet, are to be washed as white as wool it must be in the tears of a genuine contrition: our crocodile deliverances will profit us nothing. We must stop chasing dollars, stop lying, stop cheating, stop ignoring art, literature and all the refining agencies and instrumentalities of civilization. We must subdue our detestable habit of shaking hands with prosperous rascals and fawning upon the merely rich. It is not permitted to our employers to plead in justification of low wages the law of supply and demand that is giving them high profits. It is not permitted to discontented employees to break the bones of contented ones and destroy the foundations of social order. It is infamous to look upon public office with the lust of possession; it is disgraceful to solicit political preferment, to strive and compete for "honors" that are sullied and tarnished by the touch of the reaching hand. Until we amend our personal characters we shall amend our laws in vain. Though Paul plant and Apollos water, the field of reform will grow nothing but the figless thistle and the grapeless thorn. The State is an aggregation of individuals. Its public character is the expression of their personal ones. By no political prestidigitation can it be made better and wiser than the sum of their goodness and wisdom. To expect that men who do not honorably and intelligently conduct their private affairs will honorably and intelligently conduct the affairs of the community is to be a fool. We are told that out of nothing God made the Heavens and the earth; but out of nothing God never did and man never can, make a public sense of honor and a public conscience. Miracles are now performed but one day of the year--the twenty-ninth of February; and on leap year God is forbidden to perform them.

IV.

Ye who hold that the power of eloquence is a thing of the past and the orator an anachronism; who believe that the trend of political events and the results of parliamentary action are determined by committees in cold consultation and the machinations of programmes in holes and corners, consider the ascension of Bryan and be wise. A week before the convention of 1896 William J. Bryan had never heard of himself; upon his natural obscurity was superposed the opacity of a Congressional service that effaced him from the memory of even his faithful dog, and made him immune to dunning. Today he is pinnacled upon the summit of the tallest political distinction, gasping in the thin atmosphere of his unfamiliar environment and fitly astonished at the mischance. To the dizzy elevation of his candidacy he was hoisted out of the shadow by his own tongue, the longest and liveliest in Christendom. Had he held it--which he could not have done with both hands--there had been no Bryan. His creation was the unstudied act of his own larynx; it said, "Let there be Bryan," and there was Bryan. Even in these degenerate days there is a hope for the orators when one can make himself a Presidential peril by merely waving the red flag in the cave of the winds and tormenting the circumjacence with a brandish of abundant hands.

To be quite honest, I do not entirely believe that Orator Bryan's tongue had anything to do with it. I have long been convinced that personal persuasion is a matter of animal magnetism--what in its more obvious manifestation we now call hypnotism. At the back of the words and the postures, and independent of them, is that secret, mysterious power, addressing, not the ear, not the eye, nor, through them, the understanding, but through its matching quality in the auditor, captivating the will and enslaving it That is how persuasion is effected; the spoken words merely supply a pretext for surrender. They enable us to yield without loss of our self-esteem, in the delusion that we are conceding to reason what is really extorted by charm. The words are necessary, too, to point out what the orator wishes us to think, if we are not already apprised of it. When the nature of his power is better understood and frankly recognized, he can spare himself the toil of talking. The parliamentary debate of the future will probably be conducted in silence, and with only such gestures as go by the name of "passes." The chairman will state the question before the House and the side, affirmative or negative, to be taken by the honorable member entitled to the floor. That gentleman will rise, train his compelling orbs upon the miscreants in opposition, execute a few passes and exhaust his alloted time in looking at them. He will then yield to an honorable member of dissenting views. The preponderance in magnetic power and hypnotic skill will be manifest in the voting. The advantages of the method are as plain as the nose on an elephant's face. The "arena" will no longer "ring" with anybody's "rousing speech," to the irritating abridgment of the inalienable right to pursuit of sleep. Honorable members will lack provocation to hurl allegations and cuspidors. Pitchforking statesmen and tosspot reformers will be unable to play at pitch-and-toss with reputations not submitted for the performance. In short, the congenial asperities of debate will be so mitigated that the honorable member from Hades will retire permanently from the hauls of legislation.

V.

"Public opinion," says Buckle, "being the voice of the average man, is the voice of mediocrity." Is it therefore so very wise and infallible a guide as to be accepted without other credentials than its name and fame? Ought we to follow its light and leading with no better assurance of the character of its authority than a count of noses of those following it already, and with no inquiry as to whether it has not on many former occasions let them and their several sets of predecessors into bogs of error and over precipices to "eternal mock?" Surely "the average man," as every one knows him, is not very wise, not very learned, not very good; how is it that his views, of so intricate and difficult matters as those of which public opinion makes pronouncement through him are entitled to such respect? It seems to me that the average man, as I know him, is very much a fool, and something of a rogue as well. He has only a smattering of education, knows virtually nothing of political history, nor history of any kind, is incapable of logical, that is to say clear, thinking, is subject to the suasion of base and silly prejudices, and selfish beyond expression. That such a person's opinions should be so obviously better than my own that I should accept them instead, and assist in enacting them into laws, appears to me most improbable. I may "bow to the will of the people" as gracefully as a defeated candidate, and for the same reason, namely, that I can not help myself; but to admit that I was wrong in my belief and flatter the power that subdues me--no, that I will not do. And if nobody would do so the average man would not be so very cock-sure of his infallibility and might sometimes consent to be counseled by his betters.

In any matter of which the public has imperfect knowledge, public opinion is as likely to be erroneous as is the opinion of an individual equally uninformed. To hold otherwise is to hold that wisdom can be got by combining many ignorances. A man who knows nothing of algebra can not be assisted in the solution of an algebraic problem by calling in a neighbor who knows no more than himself, and the solution approved by the unanimous vote of ten million such men would count for nothing against that of a competent mathematician. To be entirely consistent, gentlemen enamored of public opinion should insist that the text books of our common schools should be the creation of a mass meeting, and all disagreements arising in the course of the work settled by a majority vote. That is how all difficulties incident to the popular translation of the Hebrew Scriptures were composed. It should be admitted, however that most of those voting knew a little Hebrew, though not much. A problem in mathematics is a very simple thing compared with many of those upon which the people are called to pronounce by resolution and ballot--for example, a question of finance.

"The voice of the people is the voice of God"--the saying is so respectably old that it comes to us in the Latin. He is a strange, an unearthly politician who has not a score of times publicly and solemnly signified his faith in it But does anyone really believe it? Let us see. In the period between 1859 and 1885, the Democratic party was defeated six times in succession. The voice of the people pronounced it in error and unfit to govern. Yet after each overthrow it came back into the field gravely reaffirming its faith in the principles that God had condemned. Then God twice reversed Himself, and the Republicans "never turned a hair," but set about beating Him with as firm a confidence of success (justified by the event) as they had known in the years of their prosperity. Doubtless in every instance of a political party's defeat there are defections, but doubtless not all are due to the voice that spoke out of the great white light that fell about Saul of Tarsus. By the way, it is worth observing that that clever gentleman was under no illusion regarding the origin of the voice that wrought his celebrated "flop"; he did not confound it with the ***vox populi*** The people of his time and place had no objection to the persecution that he was conducting, and could persecute a trifle themselves upon occasion.

Majorities rule, when they do rule, not because they ought, but because they can. We vote in order to learn without fighting which party is the stronger; it is less disagreeable to learn it that way than the other way. Sometimes the party that is numerically the weaker is by possession of the Government actually the stronger, and could maintain itself in power by an appeal to arms, but the habit of submitting when outvoted is hard to break. Moreover, we all recognize in a subconscious way, the reasonableness of the habit as a practical method of getting on; and there is always the confident hope of success in the next canvass. That one's cause will succeed because it ought to succeed is perhaps the most general and invincible folly affecting the human judgment Observation can not shake it, nor experience destroy. Though you bray a partisan in the mortar of adversity till he numbers the strokes of the pestle by the hairs of his head, yet will not this fool notion depart from him. He is always going to win the next time, however frequently and disastrously he has lost before. And he can always give you the most cogent reasons for the faith that is in him. His chief reliance is on the "fatal mistakes" made since the last election by the other party. There never was a year in which the party in power and the party out of power did not make bad mistakes--mistakes which, unlike eggs and fish, seem always worst when freshest. If idiotic errors of policy were always fatal, no party would ever win an election and there would be a hope of better government under the benign sway of the domestic cow.

VI.

Each political party accuses the "opposing candidate" of refusing to answer certain questions which somebody has chosen to ask him. I think myself it is discreditable for a candidate to answer any questions at all, to make speeches, declare his policy, or to do anything whatever to get himself elected. If a political party choose to nominate a man so obscure that his character and his views on all public questions are not known or inferable he ought to have the dignity to refuse to expound them. As to the strife for office being a pursuit worthy of a noble ambition, I do not think so; nor shall I believe that many do think so until the term "office seeker" carries a less opprobrious meaning and the dictum that "the office should seek the man, not the man the office," has a narrower currency among all manner of persons. That by acts and words generally felt to be discreditable a man may evoke great popular enthusiasm is not at all surprising. The late Mr. Barnum was not the first nor the last to observe that the people love to be humbugged. They love an impostor and a scamp, and the best service that you can do for a candidate for high political prefer-ment is to prove him a little better than a thief, but not quite so good as a thug.

VII.

The view is often taken that a representative is the same thing as a delegate; that he is to have, and can honestly entertain, no opinion that is at variance with the whims and the caprices of his constituents. This is the very ***reductio ad absur-dum*** of representative government. That it is the dominant theory of the future there can be little doubt, for it is of a piece with the progress downward which is the invariable and unbroken tendency of republican institutions. It fits in well with manhood suffrage, rotation in office, unrestricted patronage, assessment of subordinates, an elective judiciary and the rest of it. This theory of representative institutions is the last and lowest stage in our pleasant performance of "shooting Niagara." When it shall have universal recognition and assent we shall have been fairly engulfed in the whirlpool, and the buzzard of anarchy may hopefully whet his beak for the national carcass. My view of the matter--which has the further merit of being the view held by those who founded this Government--is that a man holding office from and for the people is in conscience and honor bound to do what seems to his judgment best for the general welfare, respectfully regardless of any and all other considerations. This is especially true of legislators, to whom such specific "instructions" as constituents sometimes send are an impertinence and an insult. Pushed to its logical conclusion, the "delegate" idea would remove all neces-sity of electing men of brains and judgment; one man properly connected with his constituents by telegraph would make as good a legislator as another. Indeed, as a matter of economy, one representative should act for many constituencies, receiv-ing his instructions how to vote from mass meetings in each. This, besides being logical, would have the added advantage of widening and hardening the power of the local "bosses," who, by properly managing the showing of hands could have the same beneficent influence in national affairs that they now enjoy in municipal. The plan would be a pretty good one if there were not so many other ways for the Na-tion to go to the Devil that it appears needless.

VIII.

With a wiser wisdom than was given to them, our forefathers in making the Constitution would not have provided that each House of Congress "shall be the judge of the elections, returns and qualifications of its own members." They would have foreseen that a ruling majority of Congress could not safely be trusted to exercise this power justly in the public interest, but would abuse it in the interest of party. A man's right to sit in a legislative body should be determined, not by that body, which has neither the impartiality, the knowledge of evidence nor the time to determine it rightly, but by the courts of law. That is how it is done in England, where Parliament voluntarily surrendered the right to say by whom the constituencies shall be represented, and there is no disposition to resume it. As the vices hunt in packs, so, too, virtues are gregarious; if our Congress had the righteousness to decide contested elections justly it would have also the self-denial not to wish to decide them at all.

IX

The purpose of the legislative custom of "eulogizing" dead members of Congress is not apparent unless it is to add a terror to death and make honorable and self-respecting members rather bear the ills they have than escape through the gates of death to others that they know a good deal about. If a member of that kind, who has had the bad luck to "go before," could be consulted he would indubitably say that he was sorry to be dead; and that is not a natural frame of mind in one who is exempt from the necessity of himself "delivering a eulogy."

It may be urged that the Congressional "eulogy" expresses in a general way the eulogist's notion of what he would like to have somebody say of himself when he is by death elected to the Lower House. If so, then Heaven help him to a better taste. Meanwhile it is a patriotic duty to prevent him from indulging at the public expense the taste that he has. There have been a few men in Congress who could speak of the character and services of a departed member with truth and even elo-quence. One such was Senator Vest. Of many others, the most charitable thing that one can conscientiously say is that one would a little rather hear a "eulogy" by them than on them. Considering that there are many kinds of brains and only one kind of no brains, their diversity of gifts is remarkable, but one characteristic they have in common: they are all poets. Their efforts in the way of eulogium illustrate and il-luminate Pascal's obscure saying that poetry is a particular sadness. If not sad them-selves, they are at least the cause of sadness in others, for no sooner do they take to their legs to remind us that life is fleeting, and to make us glad that it is, than they burst into bloom as poets all! Some one has said that in the contemplation of death there is something that belittles. Perhaps that explains the transformation. Anyhow the Congressional eulogist takes to verse as naturally as a moth to a candle, and with about the same result to his reputation for sense.

The poetry is commonly not his own; what it violates every law of sense, fit-ness, metre, rhyme and taste it is. But nine times in ten it is some dog's-eared, shop-worn quotation from one of the "standard" bards, usually Shakspere. There are familiar passages from that poet which have been so often heard in "the halls of legislation" that they have acquired an infamy which unfits them for publication in a decent family newspaper; and Shakspere himself, reposing in Elysium on his bed of asphodel and moly, omits them when reading his complete works to the shades of Kit Marlowe and Ben Jonson, for their sins.

This whole business ought to be "cut out" It is not only a waste of time and a sore trial to the patience of the country; it is absolutely immoral. It is not true that a member of Congress who, while living was a most ordinary mortal, becomes by the accident of death a hero, a saint, "an example to American youth." Nobody be-lieves these abominable "eulogies," and nobody should be permitted to utter them in the time and place designated for another purpose. A "tribute" that is exacted by custom and has not the fire and light of spontaneity is without sincerity or sense. A simple resolution of regret and respect is all that the occasion requires and would not inhibit any further utterance that friends and admirers of the deceased might be moved to make elsewhere. If any bereaved gentlemen, feeling his heart getting into his head, wishes to tickle his ear with his tongue by way of standardizing his emotion let him hire a hall and do so. But he should not make the Capitol a "Place of Wailing" and the Congressional Record a book of bathos.

SOME FEATURES OF THE LAW
I.

THERE is a difference between religion and the amazing circumstructure which, under the name of theology, the priesthoods have builded round about it, which for centuries they made the world believe was the true temple, and which, after incalculable mischiefs wrought, immeasurable blood spilled in its extension and consolidation, is only now beginning to crumble at the touch of reason. There is the same difference between the laws and the law--the naked statutes (bad enough, God knows) and the incomputable additions made to them by lawyers. This immense body of superingenious writings it is that we all are responsible to in person and property. It is unquestionable authority for setting aside any statute that any legislative body ever passed or can pass. In it are dictates of recognized validity for turning topsy-turvy every principle of justice and reversing every decree of reason. There is no fallacy so monstrous, no deduction so hideously unrelated to common sense, as not to receive, somewhere in the myriad pages of this awful compilation, a support that any judge in the land would be proud to recognize with a decision if ably persuaded. I do not say that the lawyers are altogether responsible for the existence of this mass of disastrous rubbish, nor for its domination of the laws. They only create and thrust it down our throats; we are guilty of contributory negligence in not biting the spoon.

As long as there exists the right of appeal there is a chance of acquittal. Otherwise the right of appeal would be a sham and an insult more intolerable, even, than that of the man convicted of murder to say why he should not receive the sentence which nothing he may say will avert. So long as acquittal may ensue guilt is not established. Why, than are men sentenced before they are proved guilty? Why are they punished in the middle of proceedings against them? A lawyer can reply to these questions in a thousand ingenious ways; there is but one answer. It is because we are a barbarous race, submitting to laws made by lawyers for lawyers. Let the "legal fraternity" reflect that a lawyer is one whose profession it is to circumvent the law; that it is a part of his business to mislead and befog the court of which he is an officer; that it is considered right and reasonable for him to live by a division of the spoils of crime and misdemeanor; that the utmost atonement he ever makes for acquitting a man whom he knows to be guilty is to convict a man whom he knows to be innocent. I have looked into this thing a bit and it is my judgment that all the methods of our courts, and the traditions of bench and bar exist and are perpetuated, altered and improved, for the one purpose of enabling the lawyers as a class to exact the greatest amount of money from the rest of mankind. The laws are mostly made by lawyers, and so made as to encourage and compel litigation. By lawyers they are interpreted and by lawyers enforced for their own profit and advantage. The whole intricate and interminable machinery of precedent, rulings, decisions, objections, writs of error, motions for new trials, appeals, reversals, affirmations and the rest of it, is a transparent and iniquitous systems of "cinching." What remedy would I propose? None. There is none to propose. The lawyers have "got us" and they mean to keep us. But if thoughtless children of the frontier sometimes rise to tar and feather the legal pelt may God's grace go with them and amen. I do not believe there is a lawyer in Heaven, but by a bath of tar and a coating of hen's-down they can be made to resemble angels more nearly than by any other process.

The matchless villainy of making men suffer for crimes of which they may eventually be acquitted is consistent with our entire system of laws--a system so complicated and contradictory that a judge simply does as he pleases, subject only to the custom of giving for his action reasons that at his option may or may not be derived from the statute. He may sternly affirm that he sits there to interpret the law as he finds it, not to make it accord with his personal notions of right and justice. Or he may declare that it could never have been the Legislature's intention to do wrong, and so, shielded by the useful phrase ***contra bonos mores***, pronounce that illegal which he chooses to consider inexpedient. Or he may be guided by either of any two inconsistent precedents, as best suits his purpose. Or he may throw aside both statute and precedent, disregard good morals, and justify the judgment that he wishes to deliver by what other lawyers have written in books, and still others, without anybody's authority, have chosen to accept as a part of the law. I have in mind judges whom I have observed to do all these things in a single term of court, and could mention one who has done them all in a single decision, and that not a very long one. The amazing feature of the matter is that all these methods are lawful--made so, not by legislative enactment, but by the judges. Language can not be used with sufficient lucidity and positiveness to land them.

The legal purpose of a preliminary examination is not the discovery of a criminal; it is the ascertaining of the probable guilt or innocence of the person already charged. To permit that person's counsel to insult and madden the various assisting witnesses in the hope of making them seem to incriminate themselves instead of him by statements that may afterward be used to confuse a jury--that is perversion of law to defeat justice. The outrageous character of the practice is seen to better advantage what contrasted with the tender consideration enjoyed by the person actually accused and presumably guilty--the presumption of his innocence being as futile a fiction as that a sheep's tail is a leg when called so. Actually, the prisoner in a criminal trial is the only person supposed to have a knowledge of the facts who is not compelled to testify! And this amazing exemption is given him by way of immunity from the snares and pitfalls with which the paths of all witnesses are wantonly beset! To a visiting Lunarian it would seem strange indeed that in a Terrestrial court of justice it is not deemed desirable for an accused person to incriminate himself, and that it *is* deemed desirable for a subpoena to be more dreaded than a warrant.

When a child, a wife, a servant, a student--any one under personal authority or bound by obligation of honor--is accused or suspected an explanation is demanded, and refusal to testify is held, and rightly held, a confession of guilt To question the accused--rigorously and sharply to examine him on all matters relating to the offense, and even trap him if he seem to be lying--that is Nature's method of criminal procedure; why in our public trials do we forego its advantages? It may annoy; a person arrested for crime must expect annoyance. It can not make an innocent man incriminate himself, not even a witness, but it can make a rogue do so, and therein lies its value. Any pressure short of physical torture or the threat of it, that can be put upon a rogue to make him assist in his own undoing is just and therefore expedient.

This ancient and efficient safeguard to rascality, the right of a witness to refuse to testify when his testimony would tend to convict him of crime, has been strengthened by a decision of the United States Supreme Court. That will probably add another century or two to its mischievous existence, and possibly prove the first act in such an extension of it that eventually a witness can not be compelled to testify at all. In fact it is difficult to see how he can be compelled to now if he has the hardihood to exercise his constitutional right without shame and with an intelligent consciousness of its limitless application.

The case in which the Supreme Court made the decision was one in which a witness refused to say whether he had received from a defendant railway company a rate on grain shipments lower than the rate open to all shippers. The trial was in the United States District Court for the Northern District of Illinois, and Judge Gresham chucked the scoundrel into jail. He naturally applied to the Supreme Court for relief, and that high tribunal gave joy to every known or secret malefactor in the country by deciding--according to law, no doubt--that witnesses in a criminal case can not be compelled to testify to anything that "*might tend* to criminate them *in any way*, or subject them to *possible* prosecution." The italics are my own and seem to me to indicate, about as clearly as extended comment could, the absolutely boundless nature of the immunity that the decision confirms or confers. It is to be hoped that some public-spirited gentleman called to the stand in some celebrated case may point the country's attention to the state of the law by refusing to tell his name, age or occupation, or answer any question whatever. And it would be a fitting *finale* to the farce if he would threaten the too curious attorney with an action for damages for compelling a disclosure of character.

Most lawyers have made so profound a study of human nature as to think that if they have shown a man to be of loose life with regard to women they have shown him to be one that would tell needless lies to a jury--a conviction unsupported by the familiar facts of life and character. Different men have different vices, and addiction to one kind of "upsetting sin" does not imply addiction to an unrelated kind. Doubtless a rake is a liar in so far as is needful to concealment, but it does not follow that he will commit perjury to save a horsethief from the penitentiary or send a good man to the gallows. As to lying, generally, he is not conspicuously worse than the mere lover, male or female; for lovers have been liars from the beginning of time. They deceive when it is necessary and when it is not. Schopenhauer says that it is because of a sense of guilt--they contemplate the commission of a crime and, like other criminals, cover their tracks. I am not prepared to say if that is the true explanation, but to the fact to be explained I am ready to testify with lifted arms. Yet no cross-examining attorney tries to break the credibility of a witness by showing that he is in love.

An habitual liar, if disinterested, makes about as good a witness as anybody. There is really no such thing as "the lust of lying:" falsehoods are told for advantage--commonly a shadowy and illusory advantage, but one distinctly enough had in mind. Discerning no opportunity to promote his interest, tickle his vanity or feed a grudge, the habitual liar will tell the truth. If lawyers would study human nature with half the assiduity that they give to resolution of hairs into their longitudinal elements they would be better fitted for service of the devil than they have now the usefulness to be.

I have always asserted the right and expediency of cross-examining attorneys in court with a view to testing their credibility. An attorney's relation to the trial is closer and more important than that of a witness. He has more to say and more opportunities to deceive the jury, not only by naked lying, but by both ***suppressio veri*** and ***suggestio falsi***. Why is it not important to ascertain his credibility; and if an inquiry into his private life and public reputation will assist, as himself avers, why should he not be put upon the grill and compelled to sweat out the desired incrimination? I should think it might give good results, for example, to compel him to answer a few questions touching, not his private life, but his professional. Somewhat like this:

"Did you ever defend a client, knowing him to be guilty?"

"What was your motive in doing so?"

"But in addition to your love of fair play had you not also the hope and assurance of a fee?"

"In defending your guilty client did you declare your belief in his innocence?"

"Yes, I understand, but necessary as it may have been (in that it helped to defeat justice and earn your fee) was not your declaration a lie?"

"Do you believe it right to lie for the purpose of circumventing justice?--yes or no?"

"Do you believe it right to lie for personal gain--yes or no?"

"Then why did you do both?"

"A man who lies to beat the laws and fill his purse is--what?"

"In defending a murderer did you ever misrepresent the character, acts, motives and intentions of the man that he murdered--never mind the purpose and effect of such misrepresentation--yes or no?"

"That is what we call slander of the dead, is it not?"

"What is the most accurate name you can think of for one who slanders the dead to defeat justice and promote his own fortune?"

"Yes, I know--such practices are allowed by the 'ethics' of your profession, but can you point to any evidence that they are allowed by Jesus Christ?"

"If in former trials you have obstructed justice by slander of the dead, by falsely affirming the innocence of the guilty, by cheating in argument, by deceiving the court whom you are sworn to serve and assist, and have done all this for personal gain, do you expect, and is it reasonable for you to expect, the jury in this case to believe you?"

"One moment more, please. Did you ever accept an annual, or other fee conditioned on your not taking any action against a corporation?"

"While in receipt of such refrainer--I beg you pardon, retainer--did you ever prosecute a blackmailer?"

It will be seen that in testing the credibility of a lawyer it is needless to go into his private life and his character as a man and a citizen: his professional practices are an ample field in which to search for offenses against man and God. Indeed, it is sufficient simply to ask him: "What is your view of 'the ethics of your profession' as a suitable standard of conduct for a pirate of the Spanish Main?"

The moral sense of the laymen is dimly conscious of something wrong in the ethics of the noble profession; the lawyers affirming, rightly enough, a public necessity for them and their mercenary services, permit their thrift to construe it vaguely as personal justification. But nobody has blown away from the matter its brumous encompassment and let in the light upon it It is very simple.

Is it honorable for a lawyer to try to clear a man that he knows deserves conviction? That is not the entire question by much. Is it honorable to pretend to believe what you do not believe? Is it honorable to lie? I submit that these questions are not answered affirmatively by showing the disadvantage to the public and to civilization of a lawyer refusing to serve a known offender. The popular interest, like any other good cause, can be and commonly is, served by foul means. Justice itself may be promoted by acts essentially unjust. In serving a sordid ambition a powerful scoundrel may by acts in themselves wicked augment the prosperity of a whole nation. I have not the right to deceive and lie in order to advantage my fellowmen, any more than I have the right to steal or murder to advantage them, nor have my fellowmen the power to grant me that indulgence.

The question of a lawyer's right to clear a known criminal (with the several questions involved) is not answered affirmatively by showing that the law forbids him to decline a case for reasons personal to himself--not even if we admit the statute's moral authority. Preservation of conscience and character is a civic duty, as well as a personal; one's fellow-men have a distinct interest in it. That, I admit, is an argument rather in the manner of an attorney; clearly enough the intent of this statute is to compel an attorney to cheat and lie for any rascal that wants him to. In that sense it may be regarded as a law softening the rigor of all laws; it does not mitigate punishments, but mitigates the chance of incurring them. The infamy of it lies in forbidding an attorney to be a gentleman. Like all laws it falls something short of its intent: many attorneys, even some who defend that law, are as honorable as is consistent with the practice of deceit to serve crime.

It will not do to say that an attorney in defending a client is not compelled to cheat and lie. What kind of defense could be made by any one who did not profess belief in the innocence of his client?--did not affirm it in the most serious and impressive way?--did not lie? How would it profit the defense to be conducted by one who would not meet the prosecution's grave asseverations of belief in the prisoner's guilt by equally grave assurances of faith in his innocence? And in point of fact, when was counsel for the defense ever known to forego the advantage of that solemn falsehood? If I am asked what would become of accused persons if they had to prove their innocence to the lawyers before making a defense in court, I reply that I do not know; and in my turn I ask: What would become of Humpty Dumpty if all the king's horses and all the king's men were an isosceles triangle?

It all amounts to this, that lawyers want clients and are not particular about the kind of clients that they get All this is very ugly work, and a public interest that can not be served without it would better be unserved.

I grant, in short, 'tis better all around
That ambidextrous consciences abound

In courts of law to do the dirty work
That self-respecting scavengers would shirk.
What then? Who serves however clean a plan
By doing dirty work, he is a dirty man.

But in point of fact I do not "grant" any such thing. It is not for the public inter-est that a rogue have the same freedom of defense as an honest man; it should be a good deal harder for him. His troubles should begin, not when he seeks acquital, but when he seeks counsel. It would be better for the community if he could not obtain the services of a reputable attorney, or any attorney at all. A defense that can not be made without his attorney's actual knowledge of his guilt should be impossible to him. Nor should he be permitted to remain off the witness stand lest he incriminate himself. It ought to be the aim of the court to let him incriminate himself--to make him do so if his testimony will. In our courts that natural method would serve the ends of justice greatly better than the one that we have. Testimony of the guilty would assist in conviction; that of the innocent would not.

As to the general question of a judge's right to inflict arbitrary punishment for words that he may be pleased to hold disrespectful to himself or another judge, I do not myself believe that any such right exists; the practice seems to be merely a survival--a heritage from the dark days of irresponsible power, when the scope of judicial authority had no other bounds than fear of the royal gout or indigestion. If in these modern days the same right is to exist it may be necessary to revive the old checks upon it by restoring the throne. In freeing us from the monarchial chain, the coalition of European Powers commonly known in American history as "the valor of our forefathers" stripped us starker than they knew.

Suppose an attorney should find his client's interests imperiled by a prejudiced or corrupt judge--what is he to do? If he may not make representations to that ef-fect, supporting them with evidence, where evidence is possible and by inference where it is not, what means of protection shall he venture to adopt? If it be urged in objection that judges are never prejudiced nor corrupt I confess that I shall have no answer: the proposition will deprive me of breath.

If contempt is not a crime it should not be punished; if a crime it should be punished as other crimes are punished--by indictment or information, trial by jury if a jury is demanded, with all the safeguards that secure an accused person against judicial blunders and judicial bias. The necessity for these safeguards is even greater in cases of contempt than in others--particularly if the prosecuting witness is to sit in judgment on his own grievance. That should, of course, not be permitted: the trial should take place before another judge.

Why should twelve able-bodied jurymen, with their oaths to guide them and the law to back, submit to the dictation of one small judge armed with nothing better than an insolent assumption of authority? A judge has not the moral right to order a jury to acquit, the utmost that he can rightly do is to point out what state of the law or facts may seem to him unfavorable to conviction. If the jurors, holding a different view, persist in conviction the accused will have grounds, doubtless, for a new trial. But under no circumstances is a judge justified in requiring a responsible human being to disregard the solemn obligation of an oath.

The public ear is dowered with rather more than just enough of clotted non-sense about "attacks upon the dignity of the Bench," "bringing the judiciary into disrepute" and the rueful rest of it. I crave leave to remind the solicitudinarians sounding these loud alarums on their several larynges that by persons of under-standing men are respected, not for what they do, but for what they are, and that one public functionary will stand as high in their esteem as another if as high in character. The dignity of a wise and righteous judge needs not the artificial safe-guarding which is a heritage of the old days when if dissent found a tongue the public executioner cut it out. The Bench will be sufficiently respected when it is no longer a place where dullards dream and rogues rob--when its *personnel* is no longer chosen in the back-rooms of tipple-shops, forced upon yawning conventions and confirmed by the votes of men who neither know what the candidates are nor what they should be. With the gang that we have and under our system must con-tinue to have, respect is out of the question and ought to be. They are entitled to just as much of its forms and observances as are needful to maintenance of order in their courts and fortification of their lawful power--no more. As to their silence under criticism, that is as they please. No body but themselves is holding their tongues.

II.

A law under which the unsuccessful respondent in a divorce proceeding may be forbidden to marry again during the life of the successful complainant, the latter being subject to no such disability, is infamous infinitely. If the disability is intended as a punishment it is exceptional among legal punishments in that it is inflicted without conviction, trial or arraignment, the divorce proceedings being quite another and different matter. It is exceptional in that the period of its continuance, and therefore the degree of its severity, are indeterminate; they are dependent on no limiting statute, and on neither the will of the power inflicting nor the conduct of the person suffering.

To sentence a person to a punishment that is to be mild or severe according to chance or--which is even worse--circumstance, which but one person, and that person not officially connected with administration of justice, can but partly control, is a monstrous perversion of the main principles that are supposed to underlie the laws.

In "the case at bar" it can be nothing to the woman--possibly herself remarried--whether the man remarries or not; that is, can affect only her feelings, and only such of them as are least creditable to her. Yet her self-interest is enlisted against him to do him incessant disservice. By merely caring for her health she increases the sharpness of his punishment--for punishment it is if he feels it such; every hour that she wrests from death is added to his "term." The expediency of preventing a man from marrying, without having the power to prevent him from making his marriage desirable in the interest of the public and vital to that of some woman, is not discussable here. If a man is ever justified in poisoning a woman who is no longer his wife it is when, by way of making him miserable, the State has given him, or he supposes it to have given him, a direct and distinct interest in her death.

III.

With a view, possibly, to promoting respect for law by making the statutes so conform to public sentiment that none will fall into disesteem and disuse, it has been advocated that there be a formal recognition of sex in the penal code, by making a difference in the punishment of men and of women for the same crimes and misdemeanors. The argument is that if women were "provided" with milder punishment juries would sometimes convict them, whereas they now commonly get off altogether.

The plan is not so new as might be thought. Many of the nations of antiquity of whose laws we have knowledge, and nearly all the European nations until within a comparatively recent time, punished women differently from men for the same offenses. And as recently as the period of the Early Puritan in New England women were punished for some offenses which men might commit without fear if not without reproach. The ducking-stool, for example, was an appliance for softening the female temper only. In England women used to be burned at the stake for crimes for which men were hanged, roasting being regarded as the milder punishment. In point of fact, it was not punishment at all, the victim being carefully strangled before the fire touched her. Burning was simply a method of disposing of the body so expeditiously as to give no occasion and opportunity for the unseemly social rites commonly performed about the scaffold of the erring male by the jocular populace. As lately as 1763 a woman named Margaret Biddingfield was burned in Suffolk as an accomplice in the crime of "petty treason." She had assisted in the murder of her husband, the actual killing being done by a man; and he was hanged, as no doubt he richly deserved. For "coining," too (which was "treason"), men were hanged and women burned. This distinction between the sexes was maintained until the year of grace 1790, after which female offenders ceased to have "a stake in the country," and like Hood's martial hero, "enlisted in the line."

In still earlier days, before the advantages of fire were understood, our good grandmothers who sinned were admonished by water--they were drowned; but in the reign of Henry III a woman was hanged--without strangulation, apparently, for after a whole day of it she was cut down and pardoned. Sorceresses and un-faithful wives were smothered in mud, as also were unfaithful wives among the ancient Burgundians. The punishment of unfaithful husbands is not of record; we only know that there were no austerely virtuous editors to direct the finger of pub-lic scorn their way.

Among the Anglo-Saxons, women who had the bad luck to be detected in theft were drowned, while men meeting with the same mischance died a dry death by hanging. By the early Danish laws female thieves were buried alive, whether or not from motives of humanity is not now known. This seems to have been the fashion in France also, for in 1331 a woman named Duplas was scourged and buried alive at Abbeville, and in 1460 Perotte Mauger, a receiver of stolen goods, was inhumed by order of the Provost of Paris in front of the public gibbet. In Germany in the good old days certain kinds of female criminals were "impaled," a punishment too grotesquely horrible for description, but likely enough considered by the simple German of the period conspicuously merciful.

It is, in short, only recently that the civilized nations have placed the sexes on an equality in the matter of the death penalty for crime, and the new system is not yet by any means universal. That it is a better system than the old, or would be if enforced, is a natural presumption from human progress, out of which it is evolved. But coincidently with its evolution has evolved also a sentiment adverse to punish-ment of women at all. But this sentiment appears to be of independent growth and in no way a reaction against that which caused the change. To mitigate the sever-ity of the death penalty for women to some pleasant form of euthanasia, such as drowning in rose-water, or in their case to abolish the death penalty altogether and make their capital punishment consist in a brief interment in a jail with a softened name, would probably do no good, for whatever form it might take, it would be, so far as woman is concerned, the "extreme penalty" and crowning disgrace, and jurors would be as reluctant to inflict it as they now are to inflict hanging.

IV.

Testators should not, from the snug security of the grave, utter a perpetual threat of disinheritance or any other uncomfortable fate to deter an American citizen, even one of his own legatees, from applying to the courts of his country for redress of any wrong from which he might consider himself as suffering. The courts of law ought to be open to any one conceiving himself a victim of injustice, and it should be unlawful to abridge the right of complaint by making its exercise more hazardous than it naturally is. Doubtless the contesting of wills is a nuisance, generally speaking, the contestant conspicuously devoid of moral worth and the verdict singularly unrighteous; but as long as some testators really *are* daft, or subject to interested suasion, or wantonly sinful, they should be denied the power to stifle dissent by fining the luckless dissenter. The dead have too much to say in this world at the best, and it is monstrous and intolerable tyranny for them to stand at the door of the Temple of Justice to drive away the suitors that themselves have made.

Obedience to the commands of the dead should be conditional upon their good behavior, and it is not good behavior to set up a censure of actions at law among the living. If our courts are not competent to say what actions are proper to be brought and what are unfit to be entertained let us improve them until they are competent, or abolish them altogether and resort to the mild and humane arbitrament of the dice. But while courts have the civility to exist they should refuse to surrender any part of their duties and responsibilities to such exceedingly private persons as those under six feet of earth, or sealed up in habitations of hewn stone. Persons no longer affectible by human events should be denied a voice in determining the character and trend of them. Respect for the wishes of the dead is a tender and beautiful sentiment, certainly. Unfortunately, it can not be ascertained that they have any wishes. What commonly go by that name are wishes once entertained by living persons who are now dead, and who in dying renounced them, along with everything else. Like those who entertained them, the wishes are no longer in existence. "The wishes of the dead," therefore, are not wishes, and are not of the dead. Why they should have anything more than a sentimental influence upon those still in the flesh, and be a factor to be reckoned with in the practical affairs of the supergraminous world, is a question to which the merely human understanding can find no answer, and it must be referred to the lawyers. When "from the tombs a doleful sound" is vented, and "thine ear" is invited to "attend the cry," an intelligent forethought will suggest that you inquire if it is anything about property. If so pass on--that is no sacred spot.

V.

Much of the testimony in French courts, civil and martial, appears to consist of personal impressions and opinions of the witnesses. All very improper and mischievous, no doubt, if--if what? Why, obviously, if the judges are unfit to sit in judgment By designating them to sit the designating power assumes their fitness--assumes that they know enough to take such things for what they are worth, to make the necessary allowances; if needful, to disregard a witness's opinion altogether. I do not know if they are fit. I do not know that they do make the needful allowances. It is by no means clear to me that any judge or juror, French, American or Patagonian, is competent to ascertain the truth when lying witnesses are trying to conceal it under the direction of skilled and conscientiousless attorneys licensed to deceive. But his competence is a basic assumption of the law vesting him with the duty of deciding. Having chosen him for that duty the French law very logically lets him alone to decide for himself what is evidence and what is not. It does not trust him a little but altogether. It puts him under conditions familiar to him--makes him accessible to just such influences and suasions as he is accustomed to when making conscious and unconscious decisions in his personal affairs.

There may be a distinct gain to justice in permitting a witness to say whatever he wants to say. If he is telling the truth he will not contradict himself; if he is lying the more rope he is given the more surely he will entangle himself. To the service of that end defendants and prisoners should, I think, be compelled to testify and denied the advantage of declining to answer, for silence is the refuge of guilt In endeavoring by austere means to make an accused person incriminate himself the French judge logically applies the same principle that a parent uses with a suspected child. When the Grandfather of His Country arraigned the wee George Washington for arboricide the accused was not carefully instructed that he need not answer if a truthful answer would tend to convict him. If he had refused to answer he would indubitably have been lambasted until he did answer, as right richly he would have deserved to be.

The custom of permitting a witness to wander at will over the entire field of knowledge, hearsay, surmise and opinion has several distinct advantages over our practice. In giving hearsay evidence, for example, he may suggest a new and important witness of whom the counsel for the other side would not otherwise have heard, and who can then be brought into court. On some unguarded and apparently irrelevant statement he may open an entirely new line of inquiry, or throw upon the case a flood of light. Everyone knows what revelations are sometimes evoked by apparently the most insignificant remarks. Why should justice be denied a chance to profit that way?

There is a still greater advantage in the French "method." By giving a witness free rein in expression of his personal opinions and feelings we should be able to calculate his frame of mind, his good or ill will to the prosecution or defense and, therefore, to a certain extent his credibility. In our courts he is able by a little solemn perjury to conceal all this, even from himself, and pose as an impartial witness, when in truth, with regard to the accused, he is full of rancor or reeking with compassion.

In theory our system is perfect. The accused is prosecuted by a public officer, who having no interest in his conviction, will serve the State without mischievous zeal and perform his disagreeable task with fairness and consideration. He is permitted to entrust his defense to another officer, whose duty it is to make a rigidly truthful and candid presentation of his case in order to assist the court to a just decision. The jurors, if there are jurors, are neither friendly nor hostile, are open-minded, intelligent and conscientious. As to the witnesses, are they not sworn to tell the truth, the whole truth (in so far as they are permitted) and nothing but the truth? What could be finer and better than all this?--what could more certainly assure justice? How close the resemblance is between this ideal picture and what actually occurs all know, or should know. The judge is commonly an ignoramus incapable of logical thought and with little sense of the dread and awful nature of his responsibility. The prosecuting attorney thinks it due to his reputation to "make a record" and tries to convict by hook or crook, even when he is himself persuaded of the defendant's innocence. Counsel for the defense is equally unscrupulous for acquittal, and both, having industriously coached their witnesses, contend against each other in deceiving the court by every artifice of which they are masters. Witnesses on both sides perjure themselves freely and with almost perfect immunity if detected. At the close of it all the poor weary jurors, hopelessly bewildered and dumbly resentful of their duping, render a random or compromise verdict, or one which best expresses their secret animosity to the lawyer they like least or their faith in the newspapers which they have diligently and disobediently read every night Commenting upon Rabelais' old judge who, when impeached for an outrageous decision, pleaded his defective eye-sight which made him miscount the spots on the dice, the most distinguished lawyer of my acquaintance seriously assured me that if all the cases with which he had been connected had been decided with the dice substantial justice would have been done more frequently than it was done. If that is true, or nearly true, and I believe it, the American's right to sneer at the Frenchman's "judicial methods" is still an open question.

It is urged that the corrupt practices in our courts of law be uncovered to public view, whenever that is possible, by dial impeccable censor, the press. Exposure of rascality is very good--better, apparently for rascals than for anybody else, for it usually suggests something rascally which they had overlooked, and so familiarizes the public with crime that crime no longer begets loathing. If the newspapers of the country are really concerned about corrupter practices than their own and willing to bring our courts up to the English standard there is something better than exposure--which fatigues. Let the newspapers set about creating a public opinion favorable to non-elective judges, well paid, powerful to command respect and holding office for life or good behavior. That is the only way to get good men and great lawyers on the Bench. As matters are, we stand and cry for what the English have and rail at the way they get it. Our boss-made, press-ridden and mob-fearing paupers and ignoramuses of the Bench give us as good a quality of justice as we merit A better quality awaits us whenever the will to have it is attended by the sense to take it.

ARBITRATION

THE universal cry for arbitration is either dishonest or unwise. For every evil there are quack remedies galore--especially for every evil that is irremediable. Of this order of remedies is arbitration, for of this order of evils is the inadequate wage of manual labor. Since the beginning of authentic history everything has been tried in the hope of divorcing poverty and labor, but nothing has parted them. It is not conceivable that anything ever will; success of arbitration, antecedently improbable, is demonstrably impossible. Most of the work of the world is hard, disagreeable work, requiring little intelligence. Most of the people of the world are unintelligent--unfit to do any other work. If it were not done by them it would not be done, and it is the basic work. Withdraw them from it and the whole superstructure would topple and fall. Yet there is too little of the work, and there are so many incapable of doing anything else that adequate return is out of the question. For the laboring *class* there is no hope of an existence that is comfortable in comparison with that of the other class; the hope of an individual laborer lies in the possibility of fitting himself for higher employment--employment of the head; not manual but cerebral labor. While selfishness remains the main ingredient of human nature (and a survey of the centuries accessible to examination shows but a slow and intermittent decrease) the cerebral workers, being the wiser and no better, will manage to take the greater profit. In justice it must be said of them that they extend a warm and sincere invitation to their ranks, and take "apprentices;" every chance of education that the other class enjoys is proof of that.

All this is perhaps a trifle abstruse; let us, then, look at arbitration more nearly; in our time it is, in form at least something new. It began as "international arbitration," which already, in settling a few disputes of no great importance, has shown itself a dangerous remedy. In the necessary negotiation to determine exactly what points to submit to whom, and how, and where, and when to submit them, and how to carry out the arbitrator's decision, scores of questions are raised, upon each of which it is as easy to disagree and fight as upon the original issue. International arbitration may be defined as the substitution of many burning questions for a smouldering one; for disputes that have reached a really acute stage are not submitted. The animosities that it has kindled have been hotter than those it has quenched.

Industrial arbitration is no better; it is manifestly worse, and any law enforcing it and enforcing compliance with its decisions, is absurd and mischievous. "Compulsory arbitration" is not arbitration, the essence whereof is voluntary submission of differences and voluntary submission to judgment. If either reference or obedience is enforced the arbitrators are simply a court with no powers to do anything but apply the law. Proponents of the fad would do well to consider this: If a party to a labor dispute is **compelled** to invoke and obey a decision of arbitrators that decision must follow strictly the line of law; the smallest invasion of any constitutional, statutory or common-law right will enable him to upset the whole judgment No legislative body can establish a tribunal empowered to make and enforce illegal or extra legal decisions; for making and enforcing legal ones the tribunals that we already have are sufficient This talk of "compulsory arbitration" is the maddest nonsense that the industrial situation has yet evolved. Doubtless it is sent upon us for our sins; but had we not already a plague of inveracity?

Arbitration of labor disputes means compromise with the unions. It can, in this country, mean nothing else, for the law would not survive a half-dozen failures to concede some part of their demands, however reasonless. By repeated strikes they would eventually get all their original demand and as much more as on second thought they might choose to ask for. Each concession would be, as it is now, followed by a new demand, and the first arbitrators might as well allow them all that they demand and all that they mean to demand hereafter.

Would not employers be equally unscrupulous. They would not. They could not afford the disturbance, the stoppage of the business, the risk of unfair decisions in a country where it is "popular" to favor and encourage, not the just, but the poor. The labor leaders have nothing to lose, not even their jobs, for their work is labor leading. Their dupes, by the way, would be dupes no longer, for with enforced arbitration the game of "follow my leader" would pay until there should be nothing to follow him to but empty treasuries of dead industries in an extinct civilization. If there must be enforced arbitration it should at least not apply to that sum of all impudent rascalities, the "sympathetic strike."

As to the men who have set up the monstrous claim asserted by the "sympathetic strike," I shall refer to the affair of 1904. If it was creditable in them to feel so much concern about a few hundred aliens in Illinois, how about the grievances of the whole body of their countrymen in California? When their employers, who they confess were good to them, were plundering the Californians, they did not strike, sympathetically nor otherwise. Year after year the railway companies picked the pockets of the Californians; corrupted their courts and legislatures; laid its Briarean hands in exaction upon every industry and interest; filled the land with lies and false reasoning; threw honest men into prisons and locked the gates of them against thieves and assassins; by open defiance of the tax collector denied to children of the poor the advantages of education--did all this and more, and these honest working men stood loyally by it, sharing in wages its dishonest gains, receivers, in one sense, of stolen goods. The groans of their neighbors were nothing to them; even the wrongs of themselves, their wives and their children did not stir them to revolt. On every breeze that blew, this great chorus of cries and curses was borne past their ears unheeded. Why did they not strike then? Where then were their fiery altruists and storm-petrels of industrial disorder? No!--the ingenious gods who have invented the Debses and Gomperses, and humorously branded them with names that would make a cat laugh, have never put it into their cold selfish hearts to order out their misguided followers to redress a public wrong, but only to inflict one--to avenge a personal humiliation, gratify an appetite for notoriety, slake a thirst for the intoxicating cup of power, or punish the crime of prosperity.

It is a practical, an illogical, a turbulent time, yes; it always is. The age of Jesus Christ was a practical age, yet Jesus Christ was sweetly impractical. In an illogical period Socrates reasoned clearly, and logically died for it. Nero's time was a time of turbulence, yet Seneca's mind was not disturbed, nor his conscience perverted. Compare their fame with the everlasting infamy that time has fixed upon the names of the Jack Cades, the Robespierres, the Tomaso Nielos--guides and gods of the "fierce democracies" which rise with a sickening periodicity to defile the page of history with a quickly fading mark of blood and fire, their own awful example their sole contribution to the good of mankind. To be a child of your time, imbued with its spirit and endowed with its aims--that is to petition Posterity for a niche in the Temple of Shame.

No strike of any prominence ever takes place in this country without the concomitants of violence and destruction of property, and usually murder. These cheerful incidents one who does not personally suffer them can endure with considerable fortitude, but the sniveling, hypocritical condemnation of them by the press that has instigated them and the strikers who have planned and executed them, and who invariably ascribe them to those whom they most injure; the solemn offers of the leaders to assist in protecting the imperiled property and avenging the dead, while openly employing counsel for every incendiary and assassin arrested in spite of them--these are pretty hard to bear. A strike means (for it includes as its main method) violence, lawlessness, destruction of the property of others than the strikers, riot and if necessary bloodshed. Even when the strikers themselves have no hand in these crimes they are morally liable for the foreknown consequences of their act. Nay, they are morally liable for ***all the*** consequences--all the inconveniences and losses to the community, all the sufferings of the poor entailed by interruptions of trade, all the privations of other workingmen whom a selfish attention to their own supposed advantage throws out of the closed industries. They are liable in morals and should be made so in law--only that strikes are needless. It is not worth while to create a multitude of complex criminal responsibilities for acts which can easily be prevented by a single and simple one. How?

First, I should like to point out that we are hearing a deal too much about a man's inalienable right to work or play, at his own sovereign will. In so far as that means--and it is always used to mean--his right to quit any kind of work at any moment, without notice and regardless of consequences to others, it is false; there is no such moral right, and the law should have at least a speaking acquaintance with morality. What is mischievous should be illegal. The various interests of civilization are so complex, delicate, intertangled and interdependent that no man, and no set of men, should have power to throw the entire scheme into confusion and disorder for pro-motion of a trumpery principle or a class advantage. In dealing with corporations we recognize that. If for any selfish purpose the trade union of railway managers had done what their sacred brakemen and divine firemen did-- had decreed that "no wheel should turn," until Mr. Pullman's men should return to work--they would have found themselves all in jail the second day. ***Their*** right to quit work was not conceded: they lacked that authenticating credential of moral and legal irresponsibility, an indurated palm. In a small lockout affecting a mill or two the offender finds a half-hearted support in ***the*** law if he is willing to pay enough deputy sheriffs; but even then he is mounted by the hobnailed populace, at its back the daily newspapers, clamoring and spitting like cats. But let the manager of a great railway discharge all its men without warning and "kill" its own engines! Then see what you will see. To commit a wrong so gigantic with impunity a man must wear overalls.

How prevent anybody from committing it? How break up this ***regime*** of strikes and boycotts and lockouts, more disastrous to others than to those at whom the blows are aimed--than to those, even, who deliver them. How make all those concerned in the management and operation of great industries, about which have grown up tangles of related and dependent interests, conduct them with some regard to the welfare of others? Before committing ourselves to the dubious and irretraceable course of "Government ownership," or to the infectious expedient of a "pension system," is there anything of promise yet untried?--anything of superior simplicity and easier application? I think so. Make a breach of labor contract by either parly to it a criminal offense punishable by imprisonment "Fine or imprisonment" will not do--the employee, unable to pay the fine, would commonly go to jail, the employer seldom. That would not be fair.

The purpose of such a law is apparent: Labor contracts would then be drawn for a certain time, securing both employer and employee and (which is more important) helpless persons in related and dependent industries--the whole public, in fact--against sudden and disastrous action by either "capital" or "labor" for accomplishment of a purely selfish or frankly impudent end. A strike or lockout compelled to announce itself thirty days in advance would be innocuous to the public, whilst securing to the party of initiation all the advantages that anybody professes to want--all but the advantage of ruining others and of successfully defying the laws.

Under the present ***regime*** labor contracts are useless; either party can violate them with impunity. They offer redress only through a civil suit for damages, and the employee commonly has nothing with which to conduct an action or satisfy a judgment. The consequence is seen in the incessant and increasing industrial disturbances, with their ever-attendant crimes against property, life and liberty--disturbances which by driving capital to investments in which it needs employ no labor, do more than all the other causes so glibly enumerated by every newspaper and politician, though by no two alike, to bring about the "hard times"--which in their turn cause further and worse disturbances.

INDUSTRIAL DISCONTENT

I.

THE time seems to have come when the two antagonistic elements of American society should, and could afford to, throw off their disguise and frankly declare their principles and purposes. But what, it may be asked, are the two antagonistic elements? Dividing lines parting the population into two camps more or less hostile may be drawn variously; for example, one may be run between the law-abiding and the criminal class. But the elements to which reference is here made are those immemorable and implacable foes which the slang of modern economics roughly and loosely distinguishes as "Capital" and "Labor." A more accurate classification--as accurate a one as it is possible to make--would designate them as those who do muscular labor and those who do not. The distinction between rich and poor does not serve: to the laborer the rich man who works with his hands is not objectionable; the poor man who does not, is. Consciously or unconsciously, and alike by those whose necessities compel them to perform it and those whose better fortune enables them to avoid it, manual labor is considered the most insufferable of human pursuits. It is a pill that the Tolstois, the "communities" and the "Knights" of Labor can not sugarcoat. We may prate of the dignity of labor; emblazon its praise upon banners; set apart a day on which to stop work and celebrate it; shout our teeth loose in its glorification--and, God help our fool souls to better sense, we think we mean it all!

If labor is so good and great a thing let all be thankful, for all can have as much of it as may be desired. The eight-hour law is not mandatory to the laborer, nor does possession of leisure entail idleness. It is permitted to the clerk, the shopman, the street peddler--to all who live by the light employment of keeping the wolf from the door without eating him--to abandon their ignoble callings, seize the shovel, the axe and the sledge-hammer and lay about them right sturdily, to the ample gratification of their desire. And those who are engaged in more profitable vocations will find that with a part of their incomes they can purchase from their employers the right to work as hard as they like in even the dullest times.

Manual labor has nothing of dignity, nothing of beauty. It is a hard, imperious and dispiriting necessity. He who is condemned to it feels that it sets upon his brow the brand of intellectual inferiority. And that brand of servitude never ceases to burn. In no country and at no time has the laborer had a kindly feeling for the rest of us, for everywhere and always has he heard in our patronising platitudes the note of contempt. In his repression, in the denying him the opportunity to avenge his real and imaginary wrongs, government finds its main usefulness, activity and justification. Jefferson's dictum that governments are instituted among men in order to secure them in "life, liberty and the pursuit of happiness" is luminous nonsense. Governments are not instituted; they grow. They are evolved out of the necessity of protecting from the handworker the life and property of the brain worker and the idler. The first is the most dangerous because the most numerous and the least content. Take from the science and the art of government, and from its methods, whatever has had its origin in the consciousness of his ill-will and the fear of his power and what have you left? A pure republic--that is to say, no government.

I should like it understood that, if not absolutely devoid of preferences and prejudices, I at least believe myself to be; that except as to result I think no more of one form of government than of another; and that with reference to results all forms seem to me bad, but bad in different degrees. If asked my opinion as to the results of our own, I should point to Homestead, to Wardner, to Buffalo, to Coal Creek, to the interminable tale of unpunished murders by individuals and by mobs, to legislatures and courts unspeakably corrupt and executives of criminal cowardice, to the prevalence and immunity of plundering trusts and corporations and the monstrous multiplication of millionaires. I should invite attention to the pension roll, to the similar and incredible extravagance of Republican and Democratic "Houses"--a plague o' them both! If addressing Democrats only, I should mention the protective tariff; if Republicans, the hill-tribe clamor for free coinage of silver. I should call to mind the existence of prosperous activity of a thousand lying secret societies having for their sole object mitigation of republican simplicity by means of pageantry and costumes grotesquely resembling those of kings and courtiers, and titles of address and courtesy exalted enough to draw laughter from an ox.

In contemplation of these and a hundred other "results," no less shameful in themselves than significant of the deeper shame beneath and prophetic of the blacker shame to come, I should say: "Behold the outcome of hardly more than a century of government by the people! Behold the superstructure whose foundations our forefathers laid upon the unstable overgrowth of popular caprice surfacing the unplummeted abysm of human depravity! Behold the reality behind our dream of the efficacy of forms, the saving grace of principles, the magic of words! We have believed in the wisdom of majorities and are fooled; trusted to the good honor of numbers, and are betrayed. Our touching faith in the liberty of the rascal, our strange conviction that anarchy making proselytes and bombs is less dangerous than anarchy with a shut mouth and a watched hand--lo, this is the beginning of the aid of the dream!"

Our Government has broken down at every point, and the two irreconcilable elements whose suspensions of hostilities are mistaken for peace are about to try their hands at each other's tempting display of throats. There is no longer so much as a pretense of amity; apparently there will not much longer be a pretense of regard for mercy and morals. Already "industrial discontent" has attained to the magnitude of war. It is important, then, that there be an understanding of principles and purposes. As the combatants will not define their positions truthfully by words, let us see if it can be inferred from the actions which are said to speak more plainly. If one of the really able men who now "direct the destinies" of the labor organizations in this country, could be enticed into the Palace of Truth and "examined" by a skilful catechist he would indubitably say something like this:

"Our ultimate purpose is abolition of the distinction between employer and employee, which is but a modification of that between master and slave.

"We propose that the laborer shall be chief owner of all the property and profits of the enterprise in which he is engaged, and have through his union a controlling voice in all its affairs.

"We propose to overthrow the system under which a man can grow richer by working with his head than with his hands, and prevent the man who works with neither from having anything at all.

"In the attainment of these ends any means is to be judged, as to its fitness for our use, with sole regard to its efficacy. We shall punish the innocent for the sins of the guilty. We shall destroy property and life under such circumstances and to such an extent as may seem to us expedient. Falsehood, treachery, arson, assassination, all these we look upon as legitimate if effective.

"The rules of 'civilized warfare' we shall not observe, but shall put prisoners to death or torture them, as we please.

"We do not recognize a non-union man's right to labor, nor to live. The right to strike includes the right to strike *him*."

Doubtless all that (and "the half is not told") sounds to the unobservant like a harsh exaggeration, an imaginative travesty of the principles of labor organizations. It is not a travesty; it has no element of exaggeration. Not in the last twenty-five years has a great strike or lockout occurred in this country without supplying facts, notorious and undisputed, upon which some of these confessions of faith are founded. The war is practically a servile insurrection, and servile insurrections are today what they ever were: the most cruel and ferocious of all manifestations of human hate. Emancipation is rough work; when he who would be free, himself strikes the blow, he can not consider too curiously with what he strikes it nor upon whom it falls. It will profit you to understand, my fine gentleman with the soft hands, the character of that which is confronting you. You are not threatened with a bombardment of roses.

Let us look into the other camp, where General Hardhead is so engrossed with his own greatness and power as not clearly to hear the shots on his picket line. Suppose we hypnotize him and make him open his "shut soul" to our searching. He will say something like this:

"In the first place, I claim the right to own and enclose for my own use or disuse as much of the earth's surface as I am desirous and able to procure. I and my kind have made laws confirming us in the occupancy of the entire habitable and arable area as fast as we can get it. To the objection that this must eventually here, as it has actually done elsewhere, deprive the rest of you places upon which legally to be born, and exclude you after surreptitious birth as trespassers from all chance to procure directly the fruits of the earth, I reply that you can be born at sea and eat fish.

"I claim the right to induce you, by offer of employment, to colonize yourselves and families about my factories, and then arbitrarily, by withdrawing the employment, break up in a day the homes that you have been years in acquiring where it is no longer possible for you to procure work.

"In determining your rate of wages when I employ you, I claim the right to make your necessities a factor in the problem, thus making your misfortunes cumulative. By the law of supply and demand (God bless its expounder!) the less you have and the less chance to get more, the more I have the right to take from you in labor and the less I am bound to give you in wages.

"I claim the right to ignore the officers of the peace and maintain a private army to subdue you when you rise.

"I claim the right to make you suffer, by creating for my advantage an artificial scarcity of the necessaries of life.

"I claim the right to employ the large powers of the government in advancing my private welfare.

"As to falsehood, treachery and the other military virtues with which you threaten me, I shall go, in them, as far as you; but from arson and assassination I recoil with horror. You see you have very little to burn, and you are not more than half alive anyhow."

That, I submit, is a pretty fair definition of the position of the wealthy man who works with his head. It seems worth while to put it on record while he is extant to challenge or verify; for the probability is that unless he mend his ways he will not much longer be wealthy, work, nor have a head.

II.

In discussion of the misdoings at Homestead and Coeur d' Alene it is amusing to observe all the champions of law and order gravely prating of "principles" and declaring with all the solemnity of owls that these sacred things have been violated. On that ground they have the argument all their own way. Indubitably there is hardly a fundamental principle of law and morals that the rioting laborers have not footballed out of the field of consideration. Indubitably, too, in doing so they have forfeited as they must have expected to forfeit, all the "moral support" for which they did not care a tinker's imprecation. If there were any question of their culpability this solemn insistence upon it would lack something of the humor with which it is now invested and which saves the observer from death by dejection.

It is not only in discussions of the "labor situation" that we hear this eternal babble of "principles." It is never out of ear, and in politics is especially clamant. Every success in an election is yawped of as "a triumph of Republican (or Democratic) principles." But neither in politics nor in the quarrels of laborers and their employers have principles a place as "factors in the problem." Their use is to supply to both combatants a vocabulary of accusation and appeal. All the fierce talk of an antagonist's violation of those eternal principles upon which organized society is founded--and the rest of it--what is it but the cry of the dog with the chewed ear? The dog that is chewing foregoes the advantage of song.

Human contests engaging any number of contestants are not struggles of principles but struggles of interests; and this is no less true of those decided by the ballot than of those in which the franker bullet gives judgment. Nor, but from considerations of prudence and expediency, will either party hesitate to transgress the limits of the law and outrage the sense of right. At Homestead and Wardner the laborers committed robbery, pillage and murder, as striking workmen invariably do when they dare, and as cowardly newspapers and scoundrel politicians encourage them in doing. But what would you have? They conceive it to be to their interest to do these things. If capitalists conceive it to be to theirs they too would do them. They do not do them for their interest lies in the supremacy of the law--under which they can suffer loss but do not suffer hunger.

"But they do murder," say the labor unions; "they bring in gangs of armed mercenaries who shoot down honest workmen striving for their rights." This is the baldest nonsense, as they know very well who utter it. The Pinkerton men are mere mercenaries and have no right place in our system, but there have been no instances of their attacking men not engaged in some unlawful prank. In the fight at Homestead the workmen were actually intrenched on premises belonging to the other side, where they had not the ghost of a legal right to be. American working men are not fools; they know well enough when they are rogues. But confession is not among the military virtues, and the question. Is roguery expedient? is not so simple that it can be determined by asking the first preacher you meet.

It would be very nice and fine all round if idle workmen would not riot nor idle employers meet force with force, but invoke the impossible Sheriff. When the Dragon has been chained in the Bottomless Pit and we are living under the rule of the saints, things will be so ordered, but in these rascal times "revolutions are not made with rosewater," and this is a revolution. What is being revolutionized is the relation between our old friends. Capital and Labor. The relation has already been altered many times, doubtless; once, we know, within the period covered by history, at least in the countries that we call civilized. The relation was formerly a severely simple one--the capitalist owned the laborer. Of the difficulty and the cost of abolishing that system it is needless to speak at length. Through centuries of time and with an appalling sacrifice of life the effort has gone on, a continuous war characterized by monstrous infractions of law and morals, by incalculable cruelty and crime. Our own generation has witnessed the culminating triumphs of this revolution, and of its three mightiest leaders the assassination of two, the death in exile of the third. And now, while still the clank of the falling chains is echoing through the world, and still a mighty multitude of the world's workers is in bondage under the old system, the others, for whose liberation was all this "expense of spirit in a waste of shame," are sharply challenging the advantage of the new. The new is, in troth, breaking down at every point The relation of employer and employee is giving but little better satisfaction than that of master and slave. The difference between the two is, indeed, not nearly so broad as we persuade ourselves to think it. In many of the industries there is practically no difference at all, and the tendency is more and more to effacement of the difference where it exists.

Labor unions, strikes and rioting are no new remedies for this insidious disorder; they were common in ancient Rome and still more ancient Egypt. In the twenty-ninth year of Rameses III a deputation of workmen employed in the Theban necropolis met the superintendent and the priests with a statement of their grievances. "Behold," said the spokesman, "we are brought to the verge of famine. We have neither food, nor oil, nor clothing; we have no fish; we have no vegetables. Already we have sent up a petition to our sovereign lord the Pharaoh, praying that he will give us these things and we are going to appeal to the Governor that we may have the wherewithal to live." The response to this complaint was one day's rations of corn. This appears to have been enough only while it lasted, for a few weeks later the workmen were in open revolt. Thrice they broke out of their quarter, rioting like mad and defying the police. Whether they were finally shot full of arrows by the Pinkerton men of the period the record does not state.

"Organized discontent" in the laboring population is no new thing under the sun, but in this century and country it has a new opportunity and Omniscience alone can forecast the outcome. Of one thing we may be very sure, and the sooner the "capitalist" can persuade himself to discern it the sooner will his eyes guard his neck: the relations between those who are able to live without physical toil and those who are not are a long way from final adjustment, but are about to undergo a profound and essential alteration. That this is to come by peaceful evolution is a hope which has nothing in history to sustain it. There are to be bloody noses and cracked crowns, and the good people who suffer themselves to be shocked by such things in others will have a chance to try them for themselves. The working man is not troubling himself greatly about a just allotment of these blessings; so that the greater part go to those who do not work with their hands he will not consider too curiously any person's claim to exemption. It would perhaps better harmonize with his sense of the fitness of things (as it would, no doubt, with that of the angels) if the advantages of the transitional period fell mostly to the share of such star-spangled impostors as Andrew Carnegie; but almost any distribution that is sufficiently objectionable as a whole to the other side will be acceptable to the distributor. In the mean time it is to be wished that the moralize, and homilizers who prate of "principles" may have a little damnation dealt out to them on account. The head that is unable to entertain a philosophical view of the situation would be notably advantaged by removal.

III.

It is the immigration of "the oppressed of all nations" that has made this country one of the worst on the face of the earth. The change from good to bad took place within a generation--so quickly that few of us have had the nimbleness of apprehension to "get it through our heads." We go on screaming our eagle in the self-same note of triumph that we were taught at our fathers' knees before the eagle became a buzzard. America is still "an asylum for the oppressed;" and still, as always and everywhere, the oppressed are unworthy of asylum, avenging upon those who give them sanctuary the wrongs from which they fled. The saddest thing about oppression is that it makes its victims unfit for anything but to be oppressed--makes them dangerous alike to their tyrants, their saviors and themselves. In the end they turn out to be fairly energetic oppressors. The gentleman in the cesspool invites compassion, certainly, but we may be very well assured, before undertaking his relief without a pole, that his conception of a prosperous life is merely to have his nose above the surface with another gentleman underfoot.

All languages are spoken in Hell, but chiefly those of Southeastern Europe. I do not say that a man fresh from the fields or the factories of Europe--even of Southeastern Europe--may not be a good man; I say only that, as a matter of fact, he commonly is not. In nine instances in ten he is a brute whom it would be God's mercy to drown on his arrival, for he is constitutionally unhappy.

Let us not deny him his grievance: he works--when he works--for men no better than himself. He is required, in many instances, to take a part of his pay in "truck" at prices of breathless altitude; and the pay itself is inadequate--hardly more than double what he could get in his own country. Against all this his howl is justified; but his rioting and assassination are not--not even when directed against the property and persons of his employers. When directed against the persons of other laborers, who choose to exercise the fundamental human right to work for whom and for what pay they please--when he denies this right, and with it the right of organized society to exist, the necessity of shooting him is not only apparent; it is conspicuous and imperative. That he and his horrible kind, of whatever nationality, are usually forgiven this just debt of nature, and suffered to execute, like rivers, their annual spring rise, constitutes the most valid of the many indictments that decent Americans by birth or adoption find against the feeble form of government under which their country groans, A nation that will not enforce its laws has no claim to the respect and allegiance of its people.

This "citizen soldiery" business is a ghastly failure. The National Guard is not worth the price of its uniforms. It is intended to be a Greater Constabulary: its purpose is to suppress disorders with which the civil authorities are too feeble to cope. How often does it do so? Nine times in ten it fraternizes with, or is cowed or beaten by the savage mobs which it is called upon to kill. In a country with a competent militia and competent men to use it there would be crime enough and some to spare, but no rioting. Rioting in a Republic is without a shadow of excuse. If we have bad laws, or if our good laws are not enforced; if corporations and capital are "tyrannous and strong;" if white men murder one another and black men outrage white women, all this is our own fault--the fault of those, among others, who seek redress or revenge by rioting and lynching. The people have always as good government, as good industrial conditions, as effective protection of person, property and liberty, as they deserve. They can have what ever they have the honesty to desire and the sense to set about getting in the right way. If as citizens of a Republic we lack the virtue and intelligence rightly to use the supreme power of the ballot so that it

> "Executes a freeman's will
> As lightning does the will of God"

we are unfit to be citizens of a Republic, undeserving of peace, prosperity and liberty, and have no right to rise against conditions due to our own moral and intellectual delinquency. There is a simple way, Messieurs the Masses to correct public evils: put wise and good men into power. If you can not do that for you are not yourselves wise, or will not for you are not yourselves good, you deserve to be oppressed when you submit and shot when you rise.

To shoot a rioter or lyncher is a high kind of mercy. Suppose that twenty-five years ago (the longer ago the better) two or three criminal mobs in succession had been exterminated in that way, "as the law provides." Suppose that several scores of lives had been so taken, including even those of "innocent spectators"--though that kind of angel does not abound in the vicinity of mobs. Suppose that no demagogue judges had permitted officers in command of the "firing lines" to be persecuted in the courts. Suppose that these events had writ themselves large and red in the public memory. How many lives would this have saved? Just as many as since have been taken and lost by rioters, plus those that for a long time to come will be taken, and minus those that were taken at that time. Make your own computation from your own data; I insist only that a rioter shot in time saves nine.

You know--you, the People--that all this is true. You know that in a Republic lawlessness is villainy entailing greater evils than it cures--that it cures none. You know that even the "money power" is powerful only through your own dishonesty and cowardice. You know that nobody can bribe or intimidate a voter who will not take a bribe or suffer himself to be intimidated--that there can be no "money power" in a nation of honorable and courageous men. You know that "bosses" and "machines" can not control you if you will not suffer then to divide you into "parties" by playing upon your credulity and senseless passions. You know all this, and know it all the time. Yet not a man has the courage to stand forth and say to your faces what you know in your hearts. Well, Messieurs the Masses, I don't consider you dangerous--not very. I have not observed that you want to tear anybody to pieces for confessing your sins, even if at the same time he confesses his own. From a considerable experience in that sort of thing I judge that you rather like it, and that he whom, secretly, you most despise is he who echoes back to you what he is pleased to think you think and flatters you for gain. Anyhow, for some reason, I never hear you speak well of newspaper men and politicians, though in the shadow of your disesteem they get an occasional gleam of consolation by speaking fairly well of one another.

CRIME AND ITS CORRECTIVES
I.

SOCIOLOGISTS have been debating the theory that the impulse to commit crime is a disease, and the ayes appear to have it--not the impulse but the decision. It is gratifying and profitable to have the point settled: we now know "where we are at," and can take our course accordingly. It has for a number of years been known to all but a few back-number physicians--survivals from an exhausted *regime*--that all disease is caused by bacilli, which worm themselves into the organs that secrete health and enjoin them from the performance of that rite. The medical conservatives mentioned attempt to whittle away the value and significances of this theory by affirming its inadequacy to account for such disorders as broken heads, sunstroke, superfluous toes, home-sickness, burns and strangulation on the gallows; but against the testimony of so eminent bacteriologists as Drs. Koch and Pasteur their carping is as that of the idle angler. The bacillus is not to be denied; he has brought his blankets and is here to stay until evicted, and eviction can not be wrought by talking. Doubtless we may confidently expect his eventual suppression by a fresher and more ingenious disturber of the physiological peace, but the bacillus is now chief among ten thousand evils and it is futile to attempt to read him out of the party.

It follows that in order to deal intelligently with the criminal impulse in our afflicted fellow-citizens we must discover the bacillus of crime. To that end I think that the bodies of hanged assassins and such persons of low degree as have been gathered to their fathers by the cares of public office or consumed by the rust of inactivity in prison should be handed over to the microscopists for examination. The bore, too, offers a fine field for research, and might justly enough be examined alive. Whether there is one general--or as the ancient and honorable orders prefer to say, "grand"--bacillus, producing a general (or grand) criminal impulse covering a multitude of sins, or an infinite number of well defined and several bacilli, each inciting to a particular crime, is a question to the determination of which the most distinguished microscopist might be proud to devote the powers of his eye. If the latter is the case it will somewhat complicate the treatment, for clearly the patient afflicted with chronic robbery will require medicines different from those that might be efficacious in a gentleman suffering from constitutional theft or the desire to represent his District in the Assembly. But it is permitted to us to hope that all crimes, like all arts, are essentially one; that murder, arson and conservatism are but different symptoms of the same physical disorder, back of which is a microbe vincible to a single medicament, albeit the same awaits discovery.

In the fascinating theory of the unity of crime we may not unreasonably hope to find another evidence of the brotherhood of man, another spiritual bond tending to draw the various classes of society more closely together.

From time to time it is said that a "wave" of some kind of crime is sweeping the country. It is all nonsense about "waves" of crime. Occasionally occurs some crime notable for its unusual features, or for the renown of those concerned. It arrests public attention, which for a time is directed to that particular kind of crane, and the newspapers, with business-like instinct, give, for a season, unusual prominence to the record of similar offenses. Then, self-deceived, they talk about a "wave," or "epidemic" of it. So far is this from the truth that one of the most noticeable characteristics of crime is the steady and unbroken monotony of its occurrence in certain forms. There is nothing so dull and unvarying as this tedious uniformity of repetition. The march of crime is never retarded, never accelerated. The criminals appear to be thoroughly well satisfied with their annual average, as shown by the periodical reports of their secretary, the statistician.

A marked illustration occurs to me. Many years ago in London a well-known and respectable gentleman was brutally garroted. It was during the "silly season"--between sessions of Parliament, when the newspapers are likely to be dull. They at once began to report cases of garroting. There appeared to be an "epidemic of garroting." The public mind was terribly excited, and when Parliament met it hastened to pass the infamous "flogging act"--a distinct reversion to the senseless and discredited methods of physical torture, so alluring to the half instructed mind of the average journalist of today. Yet the statistics published by the Home Secretary under whose administration the act was passed show that neither at the time of the alarm was there any material increase of garroting, nor in the period of public tranquillity succeeding was there any appreciable diminution.

II.

By advocating painless removal of incurable idiots and lunatics, incorrigible criminals and irreclaimable drunkards from this vale of tears Dr. W. Duncan Mc-Kim provoked many a respectable but otherwise blameless person to throw a catfit of great complexity and power. Yet Dr. McKim seemed only to anticipate the trend of public opinion and forecast its crystallization into law. It is rapidly becoming a question of not what we ought to do with these unfortunates, but what we shall be compelled to do. Study of the statistics of the matter shows that in all civilized countries mental and moral diseases are increasing, proportionately to population, at a rate which in the course of a few generations will make it impossible for the healthy to care for the afflicted. To do so will require the entire revenue which it is possible to raise by taxation--will absorb all the profits of all the industries and professions and make deeper and deeper inroads upon the capital from which they are derived. When it comes to that there can be but one result. High and humanizing sentiments are angel visitants, whom we entertain with pride and pleasure, but when *fine* entertainment becomes too costly to be borne we "speed the parting guest" forthwith. And it may happen that in inviting to his vacant place a less exciting successor--that in replacing Sentiment with Reason--we shall, in this instance, learn to our joy that we do but entertain another angel. For nothing is so heavenly as Reason; nothing is so sweet and compassionate as her voice--

"Not harsh and crabbed, as dull fools suppose,
But musical as is Apollo's lute,"

Is it cruel, is it heartless, is it barbarous to use something of the same care in breeding men and women as in breeding horses and dogs? Here is a determining question: Knowing yourself doomed to hopeless idiocy, lunacy, crime or drunkenness, would you, or would you not, welcome a painless death? Let us assume that you would. Upon what ground, then, would you deny to another a boon that you would desire for yourself?

III.

The good American is, as a rule, pretty hard upon roguery, but he atones for his austerity by an amiable toleration of rogues. His only requirement is that he must personally know the rogues. We all "denounce" thieves loudly enough, if we have not the honor of their acquaintance. If we have, why, that is different--unless they have the actual odor of the prison about them. We may know them guilty, but we meet them, shake hands with them, drink with them, and if they happen to be wealthy or otherwise great invite them to our houses, and deem it an honor to frequent theirs. We do not "approve their methods"--let that be understood; and thereby they are sufficiently punished. The notion that a knave cares a pin what is thought of his ways by one who is civil and friendly to himself appears to have been invented by a humorist. On the vaudeville stage of Mars it would probably have made his fortune. If warrants of arrest were out for every man in this country who is conscious of having repeatedly shaken hands with persons whom he knew to be knaves there would be no guiltless person to serve them.

I know men standing high in journalism who today will "expose" and bitterly "denounce" a certain rascality and tomorrow will be hobnobbing with the rascals whom they have named. I know legislators of renown who habitually in "the halls of legislation" raise their voices against the dishonest schemes of some "trust mag-nate," and are habitually seen in familiar conversation with him. Indubitably these be hypocrites all. Between the head and the heart of such a man is a wall of ada-mant, and neither organ knows what the other is doing.

If social recognition were denied to rogues they would be fewer by many. Some would only the more diligently cover their tracks along the devious paths of unrighteousness, but others would do so much violence to their consciences as to renounce the disadvantages of rascality for those of an honest life. An unworthy person dreads nothing so much as the withholding of an honest hand, the slow in-evitable stroke of an ignoring eye.

For one having knowledge of Mr. John D. Rockefeller's social life and connec-tions it would be easy to name a dozen men and women who by a conspiracy of conscription could profoundly affect the plans and profits of the Standard Oil Com-pany. I have been asked: "If John D. Rockefeller were introduced to you by a friend, would you refuse to take his hand?" I certainly should--and if ever thereafter I took the hand of that hardy "friend" it would be after his repentance and promise to re-form his ways. We have Rockefellers and Morgans because we have "respectable" persons who are not ashamed to take them by the hand, to be seen with them, to say that they know them. In such it is treachery to censure them; to cry out when robbed by them is to turn State's evidence.

One may smile upon a rascal (most of us do so many times a day) if one does not know him to be a rascal, and has not said he is; but knowing him to be, or having said he is, to smile upon him is to be a hypocrite--just a plain hypocrite or a syco-phantic hypocrite, according to the station in life of the rascal smiled upon. There are more plain hypocrites than sycophantic ones, for there are more rascals of no consequence than rich and distinguished ones, though they get fewer smiles each. The American people will be plundered as long as the American character is what it is; as long as it is tolerant of successful knavery; as long as American ingenuity draws an imaginary distinction between a man's public character and his private--his commercial and his personal In brief, the American people will be plundered as long as they deserve to be plundered. No human law can stop it, none ought to stop it, for that would abrogate a higher and more salutary law: "As ye sow ye shall reap."

In a sermon by the Rev. Dr. Parkhurst is the following: "The story of all our Lord's dealings with sinners leaves upon the mind the invariable impression, if only the story be read sympathetically and earnestly, that He always felt kindly towards the transgressor, but could have no tenderness of regard toward the transgression. There is no safe and successful dealing with sin of any kind save as that distinction is appreciated and made a continual factor in our feelings and efforts."

With all due respect for Dr. Parkhurst, that is nonsense. If he will read his New Testament more understandingly he will observe that Christ's kindly feeling to transgressors was not to be counted on by sinners of every kind, and it was not always in evidence; for example, when he flogged the money-changers out of the temple. Nor is Dr. Parkhurst himself any too amiably disposed toward the children of darkness. It is not by mild words and gentle means that he has hurled the mighty from their seats and exalted them of low degree. Such revolutions as he set afoot are not made with spiritual rose-water; there must be the contagion of a noble indignation fueled with harder wood than abstractions. The people can not be collected and incited to take sides by the spectacle of a man fighting something that does not fight back. It is men that Dr. Parkhurst is trouncing--not their crimes--not Crime. He may fancy himself "dowered with the hate of hate, the scorn of scorn," but in reality he does not hate hate but hates the hateful, and scorns, not scorn, but the scornworthy.

It is singular with what tenacity that amusing though mischievous superstition keeps its hold upon the human mind--that grave **bona fide** personification of abstractions and the funny delusion that it is possible to hate or love them. Sin is not a thing; there is no existing object corresponding to any of the mere counter-words that are properly named abstract nouns. One can no more hate sin or love virtue than one can hate a vacuum (which Nature--itself imaginary--was once by the scientists of the period solemnly held to do) or love one of the three dimensions. We may think that while loving a sinner we hate the sin, but that is not so; if anything is hated it is other sinners of the same kind, who are not quite so close to us.

"But," says Citizen Goodheart, who thinks with difficulty, "shall I throw over my friend when he is in trouble?" Yes, when you are convinced that he deserves to be in trouble; throw him all the harder and the further because he is your friend. In addition to his particular offense against society he has disgraced **you**. If there are to be lenity and charity let them go to the criminal who has foreborne to involve you in his shame. It were a pretty state of affairs if an undetected scamp, fearing exposure, could make you a co-defendant by so easy a precaution as securing your acquaintance and regard. Don't throw the first stone, of course, but when convinced that your friend is a proper target, heave away with a right hearty good-will, and let the stone be of serviceable dimensions, scabrous, textured flintwise and delivered with a good aim.

The French have a saying to the effect that to know all is to pardon all; and doubtless with an omniscient insight into the causes of character we should find the field of moral responsibility pretty thickly strewn with extenuating circumstances very suitable indeed for consideration by a god who has had a hand in besetting "with pitfall and with gin" the road we are to wander in. But I submit that universal forgiveness would hardly do as a working principle. Even those who are most apt and facile with the incident of the woman taken in adultery commonly cherish a secret respect for the doctrine of eternal damnation; and some of them are known to pin their faith to the penal code of their state. Moreover there is some reason to believe that the sinning woman, being "taken," was penitent--they usually are when found out.

I care nothing about principles--they are lumber and rubbish. What concerns our happiness and welfare, as affectible by our fellowmen, is conduct "Principles, not men," is a rogue's cry; rascality's counsel to stupidity, the noise of the duper duping on his dupe. He shouts it most loudly and with the keenest sense of its advantage who most desires inattention to his own conduct, or to that forecast of it, his character. As to sin, that has an abundance of expounders and is already universally known to be wicked. What more can be said against it, and why go on repeating that? The thing is a trifle wordworn, whereas the sinner cometh up as a flower every day, fresh, ingenious and inviting. Sin is not at all dangerous to society; it is the sinner that does all the mischief. Sin has no arms to thrust into the public treasury and the private; no hands with which to cut a throat; no tongue to wreck a reputation withal. I would no more attack it than I would attack an isosceles triangle, a vacuum, or Hume's "phantasm floating in a void." My chosen enemy must be something that has a skin for my switch, a head for my cudgel--something that can smart and ache and, if so minded, fight back. I have no quarrel with abstractions; so far as I know they are all good citizens.

THE DEATH PENALTY
I.

"DOWN with the gallows!" is a cry not unfamiliar in America. There is always a movement afoot to make odious the just principle of "a life for a life"--to represent it as "a relic of barbarism," "a usurpation of the divine authority," and the rotten rest of it The law making murder punishable by death is as purely a measure of self-defense as is the display of a pistol to one diligently endeavoring to kill without provocation. Even the most brainless opponent of "capital punishment" would do that if he knew enough. It is in precisely the same sense an admonition, a warning to abstain from crime. Society says by that law: "If you kill one of us you die," just as by display of the pistol the individual whose life is attacked says: "Desist or be shot." To be effective the warning in either case must be more than an idle threat. Even the most unearthly reasoner among the gallows-downing unfortunates would hardly expect to frighten away an assassin who knew the pistol to be unloaded. Of course these queer illogicians can not be made to understand that their position commits them to absolute non-resistance to any kind of aggression, and that is fortunate for the rest of us, for if as Christians they frankly and consistently took that ground we should be under the miserable necessity of respecting them.

We have good reason to hold that the horrible prevalence of murder in this country is due to the fact that we do not execute our laws--that the death penalty is threatened but not inflicted--that the pistol is not loaded. In civilized countries, where there is enough respect for the laws to administer them, there is enough to obey them. While man still has as much of the ancestral brute as his skin can hold widiout cracking we shall have thieves and demagogues and anarchists and assassins and persons with a private system of lexicography who define hanging as murder and murder as mischance, and many another disagreeable creation, but in all this welter of crime and stupidity are areas where human life is comparatively secure against the human hand. It is at least a significant coincidence that in these the death penalty for murder is fairly well enforced by judges who do not derive any part of their authority from those for whose restraint and punishment they hold it. Against the life of one guiltless person the lives of ten thousand murderers count for nothing; their hanging is a public good, without reference to the crimes that disclose their deserts. If we could discover them by other signs than their bloody deeds they should be hanged anyhow. Unfortunately we must have a death as evidence. The scientists who will tell us how to recognize the potential assassin, and persuade us to kill him, will be the greatest benefactor of his century.

What would these enemies of the gibbet have?--these lineal descendants of the drunken mobs that pelted the hangmen at Tyburn Tree; this progeny of criminals, which has so defiled with the mud of its animosity the noble office of public executioner that even "in this enlightened age" he shirks his high duty, entrusting it to a hidden or unnamed subordinate? If murder is unjust of what importance is it whether it's punishment by death be just or not?--nobody needs to incur it.

Men are not drafted for the death penalty; they volunteer. "Then it is not deterrent," mutters the gentleman whose rude forefather pelted the hangman. Well, as to that, the law which is to accomplish more than a part of its purpose must be awaited with great patience. Every murder proves that hanging is not altogether deterrent; every hanging that it is somewhat deterrent--it deters the person hanged. A man's first murder is his crime, his second is ours.

The voice of Theosophy has been heard in favor of downing the gallows. As usual the voice is a trifle vague and it babbles. Clear speech is the outcome of clear thought, and that is something to which Theosophists are not addicted. Considering their infirmity in that way, it would be hardly fair to take them as seriously as they take themselves, but when any considerable number of apparently earnest citizens unite in a petition to the Governor of their State, to commute the death sentence of a convicted assassin without alleging a doubt of his guilt the phenomenon challenges a certain attention to what they do allege. What these amiable persons hold, it seems, is what was held by Alphonse Karr: the expediency of abolishing the death penalty; but apparently they do not hold, with him, that the assassins should begin. They want the State to begin, believing that the magnanimous example will effect a change of heart in those about to murder. This, I take it, is the meaning of their assertion that "death penalties have not the deterring influence which imprisonment for life carries." In this they obviously err: death deters at least the person who suffers it--he commits no more murder; whereas the assassin who is imprisoned for life and immune from further punishment may with impunity kill his keeper or whomsoever he may be able to get at. Even as matters now are, the most incessant vigilance is required to prevent convicts in prison from murdering their attendants and one another. How would it be if the "life-termer" were assured against any additional inconvenience for braining a guard occasionally, or strangling a chaplain now and then? A penitentiary may be described as a place of punishment and reward; and under the system proposed the difference in desirableness between a sentence and an appointment would be virtually effaced. To overcome this objection a life sentence would have to mean solitary confinement, and that means insanity. Is that what these Theosophical gentlemen propose to substitute for death?

These petitioners call the death penalty "a relic of barbarism," which is neither conclusive nor true. What is required is not loose assertion and dogs-eared phrases, but evidence of futility, or, in lack of that, cogent reasoning. It is true that the most barbarous nations inflict the death penalty most frequently and for the greatest number of offenses, but that is because barbarians are more criminal in instinct and less easily controlled by gentle methods than civilized peoples. That is why we call them barbarous. It is not so very long since our English ancestors punished more than forty kinds of crime with death. The fact that the hangman, the boiler-in-oil and the breaker-on-the-wheel had their hands full does not show that the laws were futile; it shows that the dear old boys from whom we are proud to derive ourselves were a bad lot--of which we have abundant corroborative evidence in their brutal pastimes and in their manners and customs generally. To have restrained that crowd by the rose-water methods of modern penology--that is unthinkable.

The death penalty, say the memorialists, "creates blood-thirstiness in the unthinking masses and defeats its own ends. It is a cause of murder, not a check." These gentlemen are themselves of "the unthinking masses"--they do not know how to think. Let them try to trace and lucidly expound the chain of motives lying between the knowledge that a murderer has been hanged and the wish to commit a murder. How, precisely, does the one beget the other? By what unearthly process of reasoning does a man turning away from the gallows persuade himself that it is expedient to incur the danger of hanging? Let us have pointed out to us the several steps in that remarkable mental progress. Obviously, the thing is absurd; one might as reasonably say that contemplation of a pitted face will make a man go and catch smallpox, or the spectacle of an amputated limb on the scrap-heap of a hospital tempt him to cut off his arm.

"An eye for an eye and a tooth for a tooth," says the Theosophist, "is not justice. It is revenge and unworthy of a Christian civilization." It is exact justice: nobody can think of anything more accurately just than such punishments would be, whatever the motive in awarding them. Unfortunately such a system is not practicable, but he who denies its absolute justice must deny also the justice of a bushel of corn for a bushel of corn, a dollar for a dollar, service for service. We can not undertake by such clumsy means as laws and courts to do to the criminal exactly what he has done to his victim, but to demand a life for a life is simple, practicable, expedient and (therefore) right.

Here are two of these gentlemen's dicta, between which they inserted the one just considered, though properly they should go together in frank inconsistency:

"6. It [the death penalty] punishes the innocent a thousand times more than the guilty. Death is merciful to the tortures which the living relatives must undergo. And they have committed no crime."

"8. Death penalties have not the deterring influence which imprisonment for life carries. Mere death is not dreaded. See the number of suicides. Hopeless captivity is much more severe."

Merely noting that the "living relatives" whose sorrows so sympathetically affect these soft-hearted and soft-headed persons are those of the murderer, not those of his victim, let us consider what they really say, not what they think they say: "Death is no very great punishment, for the criminal doesn't mind it much, but hopeless captivity is a very great punishment indeed Therefore, let us spare the assassin's family the tortures they will suffer if we inflict the lighter penalty. Let us make it easier for them by inflicting the severer one."

There is sense for you!--sense of the sound old fruity Theosophical sort--the kind of sense that has lifted "The Beautiful Cult" out of the dark domain of reason into the serene altitudes of inexpressible Thrill!

As to "hopeless captivity," though, there is no such thing. In legislation, to-day can not bind tomorrow. By an act of the Legislature--even by a constitutional prohibition, we may do away with the pardoning power; but laws can be repealed, constitutions amended.

The public has a short memory, signatures to petitions in the line of mercy are had for the asking, and tender-hearted Governors are familiar afflictions. We have life sentences already, and sometimes they are served to the end--if the end comes soon enough! but the average length of "life imprisonment" is, I am told, a little more than seven years. Hope springs eternal in the human beast, and matters simply can not be so arranged that in entering the penitentiary he will "leave hope behind." Hopeless captivity is a dream.

I quote again:

"9. Life imprisonment is the natural and humane check upon one who has proven his unfitness for freedom by taking life deliberately."

What! it is no longer "much more severe" than the "relic of barbarism?" In the course of a half dozen lines of petition it has become "humane". Truly these are lightning changes of character! It would be pleasing to know just what these worthy Theosophers have the happiness to think that they think.

"It is the only punishment that receives the consent of conscience."

That is to say, their conscience and that of the convicted assassin.

"Taking the life of a murderer does not restore the life he took therefore, it is a most illogical punishment. Two wrongs do not make a right."

Here's richness! Hanging an assassin is illogical because it does not restore the life of his victim; incarceration does; therefore, incarceration is logical--***quod erat demonstrandum***.

Two wrongs certainly do not make a right, but the veritable thing in dispute is whether taking the life of a life-taker is a wrong. So naked and unashamed an example of ***petitio principii*** would disgrace a debater in a pinafore. And these wonder-mongers have the incredible effrontery to babble of "logic"! Why, if one of them were to meet a syllogism in a lonely road he would run away in a hundred and fifty directions as hard as ever he could hook it. One is almost ashamed to dispute with such intellectual cloudings.

Whatever an individual may rightly do to protect himself society may rightly do to protect him, for he is a part of itself. If he may rightly take life in defending himself society may rightly take life in defending him. If society may rightly take life in defending him it may rightly threaten to take it. Having rightly and mercifully threatened to take it, it not only rightly may take it, but expediently must.

The law of a life for a life does not altogether prevent murder. No law can altogether prevent any form of crime, nor is it desirable that it should. Doubtless God could so have created us that our sense of right and justice could have existed without contemplation of injustice and wrong, as doubtless he could so have created us that we could have felt compassion without a knowledge of suffering, but doubtless he did not. Constituted as we are, we can know good only by contrast with evil. Our sense of sin is what our virtues feed upon; in the thin air of universal morality the altar-fires of honor and the beacons of conscience could not be kept alight A community without crime would be a community without warm and elevated sentiments--without the sense of justice, without generosity, without courage, without magnanimity--a community of small, smug souls, uninteresting to God and uncoveted by the Devil. We can have too much of crime, no doubt; what the wholesome proportion is none can say. Just now we are running a good deal to murder, but he who can gravely attribute that phenomenon, or any part of it, to infliction of the death penalty, instead of virtual immunity from any penalty at all, is justly entitled to the innocent satisfaction that comes of being a simpleton.

The New Woman is against the death penalty, naturally, for she is hot and hardy in the conviction that whatever is is wrong. She has visited this world in order to straighten things about a bit, and is in distress lest the number of things be insufficient to her need. The matter is important variously; not least so in its relation to the new heaven and the new earth that are to be the outcome of woman suffrage. There can be no doubt that the vast majority of women have sentimental objections to the death penalty that quite outweigh such practical considerations in its favor as they can be persuaded to comprehend. Aided by the minority of men afflicted by the same mental malady, they will indubitably effect its abolition in the first lustrum of their political activity. The New Woman will scarcely feel the seat of power warm beneath her before giving to the assassin's "unhand me villain!" the authority of law. So we shall make again the old experiment, discredited by a thousand failures, of preventing crime by tenderness to caught criminals. And the criminal uncaught will treat us to a quality of toughness notably augmented by the Christian spirit of the regime.

II.

As to painless executions, the simple and practical way to make them both just and popular is the adoption by murderers of a system of painless assassinations. Until this is done there seems to be no hope that the people will renounce the wholesome discomfort of the style of executions endeared to them by memories and associations of the tenderest character. There is also, I fancy, a shaping notion in the public mind that the penologists and their allies have gone about as far as they can safely be permitted to go in the direction of a softer suasion of the criminal nature toward good behavior. The modern prison has become a rather more comfortable habitation than the dangerous classes are accustomed to at home. Modern prison life has in their eyes something of the charm and glamor of an ideal existence, like that in the Happy Valley from which Rasselas had the folly to escape. Whatever advantages to the public may be secured by abating the rigors of imprisonment and inconveniences incident to execution, there is this objection, it makes them less deterrent. Let the penologers and philanthrope, have their way and even hanging might be made so pleasant and withal so interesting a social distinction that it would deter nobody but the person hanged. Adopt the euthanasian method of electricity, asphyxia by smothering in rose-leaves, or slow poisoning with rich food, and the death penalty may come to be regarded as the object of a noble ambition to the **bon vivant**, and the rising young suicide may go and murder somebody else instead of himself in order to receive a happier dispatch than his own 'prentice hand can assure him.

But the advocates of agreeable pains and penalties tell us that in the darker ages, when cruel and degrading punishment was the rule, and was freely inflicted for every light infraction of the law, crime was more common than it is now; and in this they appear to be right. But they one and all overlook a fact equally obvious and vastly significant: that the intellectual, moral and social condition of the masses was very low. Crime was more common because ignorance was more common, poverty was more common, sins of authority, and therefore hatred of authority, were more common. The world of even a century ago was a quite different world from the world of today, and a vastly more uncomfortable one. The popular adage to the contrary notwithstanding, human nature was not by a long cut the same then that it is now. In the very ancient time of that early English king, George III, when women were burned at the stake in public for various offenses and men were hanged for "coining" and children for theft, and in the still remoter period, (circa 1530) when poisoners were boiled in several waters, divers sorts of criminals were disemboweled and some are thought to have undergone *the pene forte et dure* of cold-pressing (an infliction which the pen of Hugo has since made popular--in literature)--in these wicked old days it is possible that crime flourished, not because of the law's severity, but in spite of it. It is possible that our respected and respectable ancestors understood the situation as it then was a trifle better than we can understand it on the hither side of this gulf of years, and that they were not the reasonless barbarians that we think them to have been. And if they were, what must have been the unreason and barbarity of the criminal element with which they had to deal?

I am far from thinking that severity of punishment can have the same restraining effect as probability of some punishment being inflicted; but if mildness of penalty is to be superadded to difficulty of conviction, and both are to be mounted upon laxity in detection, the "pile" will be "complete" with a vengeance. There is a peculiar fitness, perhaps, in the fact that all these ideas for comfortable punishment should be urged at a time when there appears to be a tolerably general disposition to inflict no punishment at all. There are, however, still a few old-fashioned persons who hold it obvious that one who is ambitious to break the laws of his country will not with as light a heart and as airy an indifference incur the peril of a harsh penalty as he will the chance of one more nearly resembling that which he would select for himself.

III.

After lying for more than a century dead I was revived, given a new body, and restored to society. This was in the year 2015. The first thing of interest that I observed was an enormous building, covering a square mile of ground. It was surrounded on all sides by a high, strong wall of hewn stone upon which armed sentinels paced to and fro. In one face of the wall was a single gate of massive iron, strongly guarded. While admiring the cyclopean architecture of the "reverend pile" I was accosted by a man in uniform, evidently The Warden, with a cheerful salutation.

"Colonel," I said, pressing his hand, "it gives me pleasure to find some one that I can believe. Pray tell me what is this building."

"That," said the colonel, "is the new State penitentiary. It is one of twelve, all alike."

"You surprise me," I replied. "Surely the criminal element must have increased enormously."

"Yes, indeed," he assented; "under the Reform *regime*, which began in your day, it became so powerful, bold and fierce that arrests were no longer possible and the prisons then in existence were soon overcrowded. The State was compelled to erect others of greater capacity."

"But, Colonel," I protested, "if the criminals were too bold and powerful to be taken into custody, of what use are the prisons! And how are they crowded?"

He fixed upon me a look that I could not fail to interpret as expressing a doubt of my sanity. "What?" he said, "is it possible that the modern Penology is unknown to you? Do you suppose we practise the antiquated and ineffective method of shutting up the rascals? Sir, the growth of the criminal element has, as I said, compelled the erection of more and larger prisons. We have enough to hold comfortably all the honest men and women of the State. Within these protecting walls they carry on all the necessary vocations of life excepting commerce. That is necessarily in the hands of the rogues as before."

"Venerated representative of Reform," I exclaimed, wringing his hand with effusion, "you are Knowledge, you are History, you are the Higher Education! We must talk further. Come, let us enter this benign edifice; you shall show me your dominion and instruct me in the rules. You shall propose me as an inmate."

I walked rapidly to the gate. When challenged by the sentinel, I turned to summon my instructor. He was nowhere visible: desolate and forbidding, as about the broken statue of Ozymandias,

"The lone and level sands stretched far away."

RELIGION
I.

This is my ultimate and determining test of right--"What, in the circumstanc-es, would Christ have done?"--the Christ of the New Testament, not the Christ of the commentators, theologians, priests and parsons. The test is perhaps not infal-lible, but it is exceedingly simple and gives as good practical results as any. I am not a Christian, but so far as I know, the best and truest and sweetest character in literature, is next to Buddha, Jesus Christ. He taught nothing new in goodness, for all goodness was ages old before he came; but with an almost infallible intuition he applied to life and conduct the entire law of righteousness. He was a lightning moral calculator: to his luminous intelligence the statement of the problem car-ried the solution--he could not hesitate, he seldom erred. That upon his deeds and words was founded a religion which in a debased form persists and even spreads to this day is mere attestation of his marvelous gift: adoration is a primitive mode of recognition.

It seems a pity that this wonderful man had not a longer life under more com-plex conditions--conditions more nearly identical with those of the modern world and the future. One would like to be able to see, through the eyes of his biogra-phers, his genius applied to more and more difficult questions. Yet one can hardly go wrong in inference of his thought and act. In many of the complexities and en-tanglements of modern affairs it is no easy matter to find an answer off-hand to the question,"What is it right to do?" But put it in another way: "What would Christ have done?" and lo! there is light. I Doubt spreads her bat-like wings and is away; the sun of truth springs into the sky, splendoring the path of right and marking that of error with a deeper shade.

II.

Gentlemen of the secular press dealt with the Rev. Mr. Sheldon not altogether fairly. To some very relevant considerations they gave no weight. It was not fair, for example, to say, as the distinguished editor of the "North American Review" did, that in professing to conduct a daily newspaper for a week as he conceived that Christ would have conducted it, Mr. Sheldon acted the part of "a notoriety seeking mountebank." It seldom is fair to go into the question of motive, for that is something upon which one has the least light, even when the motive is one's own. The motives that we think dominale us seem simple and obvious; they are in most instances exceedingly complex and obscure. Complacently surveying the wreck and ruin that he has wrought, even that great anarch, the "well meaning person," can not have entire assurance that he meant as well as the disastrous results appear to him to show.

The trouble with Mr. Harvey of the "Review" was inability to put himself in another's place if that happened to be at any considerable distance from his own place. He made no allowance for the difference in the point of view--for the difference, that is, between his mind and the mind of Mr. Sheldon. If Mr. Harvey had undertaken to conduct that Kansas newspaper as Christ would have done he would indeed have been "a notoriety seeking mountebank," or some similarly unenviable thing, for only a selfish purpose could persuade him to an obviously resultless work. But Mr. Sheldon was different--his was the religious mind--a mind having faith in an "overruling" Providence who can, and frequently does, interfere with the orderly relation of cause and effect, accomplishing an end by means otherwise inadequate to its production. Believing himself a faithful servant of that Power, and asking daily for its interposition for promotion of a highly moral purpose, why should he not have expected his favor to the enterprise? To expect that was, in Mr. Sheldon, natural, reasonable, wise; his folly lay in believing in conditions making it expectable. A person convinced that the law of gravitation is suspended is no fool for walking into a bog. Mr. Harvey may understand, but Mr. Sheldon can not understand, that Jesus Christ would not edit a newspaper at all.

The religious mind, it should be understood, is not logical. It may acquire, as Whateley's did, a certain familiarity with the syllogism as an abstraction, but of the syllogism's practical application, its real relation to the phenomena of thought, the religious mind can know nothing. That is merely to say that the mind congenitally gifted with the power of logic and accessible to its light and leading does not take to religion, which is a matter, not of reason, but of feeling--not of the head, but of the heart. Religions are conclusions for which the facts of nature supply no major premises. They are accepted or rejected according to the original mental make-up of the person to whom they appeal for recognition. Believers and unbelievers are like two boys quarreling across a wall. Each got to his place by means of a ladder. They may fight if they will, but neither can kick away the other's support.

Believing the things that he did believe, Mr. Sheldon was entirely right in thinking that the main purpose of a newspaper should be the salvation of souls. If his religious belief is true that should be the main purpose, not only of a newspaper, but of everything that has a purpose, or can be given one. If we have immortal souls and the consequences of our deeds in the body reach over into another life in another world, determining there our eternal state of happiness or pain, that is the most momentous fact conceivable. It is the only momentous fact; all others are chaff and rags. A man who, believing it to be a fact, does not make it the one purpose of his life to save his soul and the souls of others that are willing to be saved is a fool and a rogue. If he think that any part of this only needful work can be done by turning a newspaper into a gruelpot he ought to do so or (preferably) perish in the attempt.

The talk of degrading the sacred name, and all that, is mostly nonsense. If one may not test his conduct in this life by reference to the highest standard that his religion affords it is not easy to see how religion is to be made anything but a mere body of doctrine. I do not think the Christian religion will ever be seriously discredited by an attempt to determine, even with too dim a light, what under given circumstances, the man miscalled its "founder" would do. What else is his great example good for? But it is not always enough to ask oneself, "How would Christ do this?" One should first consider whether Christ would do it. It is conceivable that certain of his thrifty contemporaries may have asked him how he would change money in the Temple.

If Mr. Sheldon's critics were unfair his defenders were, as a rule, not much better. They meant to be fair, but they had to be foolish. For example, there is the Rev. Dr. Parkhurst, whose defence was published with Mr. Harvey's attack. I shall give a single illustration of how this more celebrated than cerebrated "divine" is pleased to think that he thinks. He is replying to some one's application to this matter of

Christ's injunction, "Lay not up for yourselves treasures on earth." This command, he gravely says, "is not against money, nor against the making of money, but against the loving it for its own sake and the dedicating of it to self-aggrandizing uses." I call this a foolish utterance, because it violates the good old rule of not telling an obvious falsehood. In no word nor syllable does Christ's injunction give the least color of truth to the reverend gentleman's "interpretation;" that is the reverend gentleman's very own, and doubtless he feels an honest pride in it. It is the product of a controversial need--a characteristic attempt to crawl out of a hole in an enclosure which he was not invited to enter. The words need no "interpretation;" are capable of none; are as clear and unambiguous a proposition as language can frame. Moreover, they are consistent with all that we think we know of their author's life and character, for he not only lived in poverty and taught poverty as a blessing, but commanded it as a duty and a means of salvation. The probable effect of universal obedience among those who adore him as a god is not at present an urgent question. I think even so faithful a disciple as the Rev. Dr. Parkhurst has still a place to lay his head, a little of the wherewithal to be clothed, and a good deal of the power of interpretation to excuse it.

III.

There are other hypocrites than those of the pulpit Dr. Gatling, the ingenious scoundrel who invented the gun that bears his name with commendable fortitude, says he has given much thought to the task of bringing the forces of war to such perfection that war will be no more. Commonly the man who talks of war becoming so destructive as to be impossible is only a harmless lunatic, but this fellow utters his cant to conceal his cupidity. If he thought there was any danger of the nations beating their swords into plowshares we should see him "take the stump" against agriculture forthwith. The same is true of all military inventors. They are lions' parasites; themselves, of cold blood they fatten upon hot. The sheep-tick's paler fare is not at all to their taste.

I sometimes wish I were a preacher: preachers do so blindly ignore their shining opportunities. I am indifferently versed in theology--whereof, so help me Heaven,

I do not believe one word--but know something of religion. I know, for example, that Jesus Christ was no soldier; that war has two essential features which did not command His approval: aggression and defence. No man can either attack or defend and remain Christian; and if no man, no nation. I could quote texts by the hour proving that Christ taught not only absolute abstention from violence but absolute non-resistance. Now what do we see? Nearly all the so-called Christian nations of the world sweating and groaning under their burdens of debt contracted in violation of these injunctions which they believe divine--contracted in perfecting their means of offense and defense. "We must have the best," they cry; and if armor plates for ships were better when alloyed with silver, and guns if banded with gold, such armor plates would be put upon the ships, such guns would be freely made. No sooner does one nation adopt some rascal's costly device for taking life or protecting it from the taker (and these soulless inventors will as readily sell the product of their malign ingenuity to one nation as to another) than all the rest either possess themselves of it or adopt something superior and more expensive; and so all pay the penalty for the sins of each. A hundred million dollars is a moderate estimate of what it has cost the world to abstain from strangling the infant Gatling in his cradle.

You may say, if you will, that primitive Christianity--the Christianity of Christ--is not adapted to these rough-and-tumble times; that it is not a practical scheme of conduct. As you please; I have not undertaken to say what it is not, but what it partly is. I am no Christian, though I think that Christ probably knew what was good for man about as well as Dr. Gatling or the United States Ordnance Office. It is not for me to defend Christianity; Christ did not. Nevertheless, I can not forbear the wish that I were a preacher, in order sincerely to affirm that the awful burdens borne by modern nations are obvious judgments of Heaven for disobedience to the Prince of Peace. What a striking theme to kindle fires upon the heights of imagination--to fill the secret sources of eloquence--to stir the very stones in the temple of truth! What a noble subject for the pious gentlemen who serve (with rank, pay and allowances) as chaplains in the Army and the Navy, or the civilian divines who offer prayer at the launching of an ironclad!

IV.

A matter of missionaries commonly is to the fore as a cause of quarrel among nations which have the hardihood to prefer their own religions to ours. Missionaries constitute, in truth, a perpetual menace to the national peace. I dare say the most of them are conscientious men and women of a certain order of intellect. They believe, and from the way that they interpret their sacred book have some reason to believe, that in meddling uninvited with the spiritual affairs of others they perform a work acceptable to God--their God. They think they discern a moral difference between "approaching" a man of another religion about the state of his soul and approaching him on the condition of his linen or the character of his wife. I think there is no difference. I have observed that the person who volunteers an interest in my spiritual welfare is the same person from whom I must expect an impudent concern about my temporal affairs. The missionary is one who goes about throwing open the shutters of other men's bosoms in order to project upon the blank walls a shadow of himself.

No ruler nor government of sense would willingly permit foreigners to sap the foundation of the national religion. No ruler nor government ever does permit it except under the stress of compulsion. It is through the people's religion that a wise government governs wisely--even in our own country we make only a transparent pretense of officially ignoring Christianity, and a pretense only because we have so many kinds of Christians, all jealous and inharmonious. Each sect would make this a Theocracy if it could, and would that make short work of any missionary from abroad. Happily all religions but ours have the sloth and timidity of error; Christianity alone, drawing vigor from eternal truth, is courageous enough and energetic enough to make itself a nuisance to people of every other faith. The Jew not only does not bid for converts, but discourages them by imposition of hard conditions, and the Moslem True Believer's simple, forthright method of reducing error is to cut off the head holding it. I don't say that this is right; I say only that, being practical and comprehensible, it commands a certain respect from the impartial observer not conversant with scriptural justification of the other practice.

It is only where the missionaries have made themselves hated that there is any molestation of Europeans engaged in the affairs of this world. Chinese antipathy to Caucasians in China is neither a racial animosity nor a religious; it is an instinctive dislike of persons who will not mind their own business. China has been infested with missionaries from the earliest centuries of our era, and they have rarely been molested when they have taken the trouble to behave themselves. In the time of the Emperor Justinian the fact that the Christian religion was openly preached throughout China enabled that sovereign to wrest from the Chinese the jealously-guarded secret of silk-making. He sent two monks to Pekin, who alternately preached seriousness and studied sericulture, and who brought away silkworms' eggs concealed in sticks.

In religious matters the Chinese are more tolerant than we. They let the religions of others alone, but naturally and rightly demand that others shall let theirs alone. In China, as in other Oriental countries where the color line is not drawn and where slavery itself is a light affliction, the mental attitude of the zealot who finds gratification in "spreading the light" of which he deems himself custodian, is not understood. Like most things not understood, it is felt to be bad, and is indubitably offensive.

V.

At a church club meeting a paper was read by a minister entitled, "Why the Masses Do not Attend the Churches." This good and pious man was not ashamed to account for it by the fact that there is no Sunday law, and "the masses" can find recreation elsewhere, even in the drinking saloons. It is frank of him to admit that he and his professional brethren have not brains enough to make religious services more attractive than shaking dice for cigars or playing cards for drink; but if it is a fact he must not expect the local government to assist in spreading the gospel by rounding-up the people and corralling them in the churches. The truth is, and this gentleman suspects it, that "the masses" stay out of hearing of his pulpit because he talks nonsense of the most fatiguing kind; they would rather do any one of a thousand other things than go to hear it. These parsons are like a scolding wife who grieves because her husband will not pass his evenings with her. The more she grieves, the more she scolds and the more diligently he keeps away from her. I don't think Jack Satan is conspicuously wise, but he is in the main a good entertainer, with a right pretty knack at making people come again; but the really reprehensible part of his performance is not the part that attracts them. The parsons might study his methods with great advantage to religion and morality.

It may be urged that religious services have not entertainment for their object. But the people, when not engaged in business or labor, have it for *their* object. If the clergy do not choose to adapt their ministrations to the characters of those to whom they wish to minister, that is their own affair; but let them accept the consequences. "The masses" move along the line of least reluctance. They do not really enjoy Sunday at all; they try to get through the day in the manner that is least wearisome to the spirit. Possibly their taste is not what it ought to be. If this minister were a physician of bodies instead of souls, and patients who had not called him in should refuse to take the medicine which he thought his best and they his nastiest, he should either offer them another, a little less disagreeable if a little less efficacious, or let them alone. In no case is he justified in asking the civil authority to hold their noses while he plies the spoon.

"The masses" have not asked for churches and services; they really do not care for anything of the kind--whether they ought is another matter. If the clergy choose to supply them, that is well and worthy. But they should understand their relation to the impenitent worldling, which is precisely that of a physician without a mandate from the patient, who may not be convinced that there is very much the matter with him. The physician may have a diploma and a State certificate authorizing him to practise, but if the patient do not deem himself bound to be practised upon has the physician a right to make him miserable until he will submit? Clearly, he has not. If he can not persuade him to come to the dispensary and take medicine there is an end to the matter, and he may justly conclude that he is misfitted to his vocation.

I am sure that the ministers and that singularly small contingent of earnest and, on the whole, pretty good persons who cluster about them do not perceive how alien they are in their convictions, tastes, sympathies and general mental habitudes to the great majority of their fellow men and women. Their voices, like "the gushing wave" which, to the ears of the lotus-eaters,

"Far, far away did seem to mourn and rave,"

come to us as from beyond a great gulf--mere ghosts of sound, almost destitute of signification. We know that they would have us do something, but what it is we do not clearly apprehend. We feel that they are concerned for us, but why we are imperfectly able to conceive. In an intelligible tongue they tell us of unthinkable things. Here and there in the discourse we catch a word, a phrase, a sentence--something which, from ancestors whose mother-speech it was, we have inherited the capacity to understand; but the homily as a whole is devoid of meaning. Solemn and sonorous enough it all is, and not unmusical, but it lacks its natural accompaniment of shawm and sackbut and the wind-swept harp in the willows by the waters of Babylon. It is, in fact, something of a survival--the memory of a dream.

VI.

The first week of January is set apart as a week of prayer. It is a custom of more than a half century's age, and it seems that "gracious answers have been received in proportion to the earnestness and unanimity of the petitions." That is to say, in this world's speech, the more Christians that have prayed and the more they have meant it, the better the result is known to have been. I don't believe all that. I don't believe that when God is asked to do something that he had not intended to do he counts noses before making up his mind whether to do it or not God probably knows the character of his work, and knowing that he has made this a world of knaves and dunces he must know that the more of them that ask for something, and the more loudly they ask, the stronger is the presumption that they ought not to have it. And I think God is perhaps less concerned about his popularity than some good folk seem to suppose.

Doubtless there are errors in the record of results--some things set down as "answers" to prayer which came about through the orderly operation of natural laws and would have occurred anyhow. I am told that similar errors have been made, or are believed to have been made, in the past. In 1730, for example, a good Bishop at

Auvergne prayed for an eclipse of the sun as a warning to unbelievers. The eclipse ensued and the pious prelate made the most of it; but when it was shown that the astronomers of the period had foretold it he was a sufferer from irreverent gibes. A monk of Treves prayed that an enemy of the church, then in Paris, might lose his head, and it fell off; but it transpired that, unknown (or known) to the monk, the man was under sentence of decapitation when the prayer was made. This is related by Ausolus, who piously explains, however, that but for the prayer the sentence might perhaps have been commuted to service in the galleys. I have myself known a minister to pray for rain, and the rain came. Perhaps you can conceive his discomfiture when I showed him that the weather bureau had previously predicted a fair day.

I do not object to a week of prayer. But why only a week? If prayer is "answered" Christians ought to pray all the time. That prayer is "answered" the Scripture affirms as positively and unequivocally as anything can be affirmed in words: "All things whatsoever ye shall ask in prayer, believing, that ye shall receive." Why, then, when all the clergy of this country prayed, publicly for the recovery of President McKinley, did the man die? Why is it that although two pious Chaplains ask almost daily that goodness and wisdom may descend upon Congress, Congress remains wicked and unwise? Why is it that although in all the churches and half the dwellings of the land God is continually asked for good government, good government remains what it always and everywhere has been, a dream? From Earth to Heaven in unceasing ascension flows a stream of prayer for every blessing that man desires, yet man remains unblest, the victim of his own folly and passions, the sport of fire, flood, tempest and earthquake, afflicted with famine and disease, war, poverty and crime, his world an incredible welter of evil, his life' a labor and his hope a lie. Is it possible that all this praying is futilized and invalidated by the lack of faith?--that the "asking" is not credentialed by the "believing?" When the anointed minister of Heaven spreads his palms and uprolls his eyes to beseech a general blessing or some special advantage is he the celebrant of a hollow, meaningless rite, or the dupe of a false promise? One does not know, but if one is not a fool one does know that his every resultless petition proves him by the inexorable laws of logic to be the one or the other.

VII.

Modern Christianity is beautiful exceedingly, and he who admires not is eyed batly and minded as the mole. "Sell all thou hast," said Christ and "give to the poor." All--no less--in order "to be saved." The poor were Christ's peculiar care. Ever for them and their privations, and not greatly for their spiritual darkness, fell from his lips the compassionate word, the mandate divine for their relief and cherishing. Of foreign missions, of home missions, of mission schools, of church buildings, of work among pagans *in partibus infidelium*, of work among sailors, of communion table, of delegates to councils--of any of these things he knew no more than the moon man. They were inventions of others, as is the entire florid and flamboyant fabric of ecclesiasticism that has been reared, stone by stone and century after century, upon his simple life and works and words. "Founder," indeed! He founded nothing, instituted nothing; Paul did all that Christ simply went about doing, and being, good-- admonishing the rich, whom he regarded as criminals, comforting the luckless and uttering wisdom with that Oriental indirection wherein our stupid ingenuity finds imaginary warrant for all desiderated pranks and fads.

IMMORTALITY

THE desire for life everlasting has commonly been affirmed to be universal-- at least that is the view taken by those unacquainted with Oriental faiths and with Oriental character. Those of us whose knowledge is a trifle wider are not prepared to say that the desire is universal or even general.

If the devout Buddhist, for example, wishes to "live alway," he has not succeeded in very clearly formulating the desire. The sort of thing that he is pleased to hope for is not what we should call life, and not what many of us would care for.

When a man says that everybody has "a horror of annihilation," we may be very sure that he has not many opportunities for observation, or that he has not availed himself of all that he has. Most persons go to sleep rather gladly, yet sleep is virtual annihilation while it lasts; and if it should last forever the sleeper would be no worse off after a million years of it than after an hour of it There are minds sufficiently logical to think of it that way, and to them annihilation is not a disagreeable thing to contemplate and expect.

In this matter of immortality, people's beliefs appear to go along with their wishes. The chap who is content with annihilation thinks he will get it; those that want immortality are pretty sure they are immortal, and that is a very comfortable allotment of faiths. The few of us that are left unprovided for are those who don't bother themselves much about the matter, one way or another.

The question of human immortality is the most momentous that the mind is capable of conceiving. If it is a fact that the dead live, all other facts are in comparison trivial and without interest. The prospect of obtaining certain knowledge with regard to this stupendous matter is not encouraging. In all countries but those in barbarism the powers of the profoundest and most penetrating intelligences have been ceaselessly addressed to the task of glimpsing a life beyond this life; yet today no one can truly say that he knows. It is still as much a matter of faith as ever it was.

Our modern Christian nations hold a passionate hope and belief in another world, yet the most popular writer and speaker of his time, the man whose lectures drew the largest audiences, the work of whose pen brought him the highest rewards, was he who most strenuously strove to destroy the ground of that hope and unsettle the foundations of that belief.

The famous and popular Frenchman, Professor of Spectacular Astronomy, Camille Flammarion, affirms immortality because he has talked with departed souls who said that it was true. Yes, Monsieur, but surely you know the rule about hearsay evidence. We Anglo-Saxons are very particular about that. Your testimony is of that character.

"I don't repudiate the presumptive arguments of school men. I merely supplement them with something positive. For instance, if you assumed the existence of God this argument of the scholastics is a good one. God has implanted in all men the desire of perfect happiness. This desire can not be satisfied in our lives here. If there were not another life wherein to satisfy it then God would be a deceiver. ***Voila tout***."

There is more: the desire of perfect happiness does not imply immortality, even if there is a God, for:

(1) God may not have implanted it, but merely suffers it to exist, as He suffers sin to exist, the desire of wealth, the desire to live longer than we do in this world. It is not held that God implanted all the desires of the human heart. Then why hold that He implanted that of perfect happiness?

(2) Even if He did--even if a divinely implanted desire entail its own gratifica-tion--even if it can not be gratified in this life--that does not imply immortality. It implies **only** another life long enough for its gratification just once. An eternity of gratification is not a logical inference from it.

(3) Perhaps God *is* "a deceiver" who knows that He is not? Assumption of the existence of a God is one thing; assumption of the existence of a God who is honor-able and candid according to our finite conception of honor and candor is another.

(4) There may be an honorable and candid God. He may have implanted in us the desire of perfect happiness. It may be--it is--impossible to gratify that desire in this life. Still, another life is not implied, for God may not have intended us to draw the inference that He is going to gratify it. If omniscient and omnipotent, God must be held to have intended, whatever occurs, but no such God is assumed in M. Flam-marion's illustration, and it may be that God's knowledge and power are limited, or that one of them is limited.

M. Flammarion is a learned, if somewhat "yellow" astronomer.

He has a tremendous imagination, which naturally is more at home in the mar-velous and catastrophic than in the orderly regions of familiar phenomena. To him the heavens are an immense pyrotechnicon and he is the master of the show and sets off the fireworks. But he knows nothing of logic, which is the science of straight thinking, and his views of things have therefore no value; they are nebulous.

Nothing is clearer than that our pre-existence is a dream, having absolutely no basis in anything that we know or can hope to know. Of after-existence there is said to be evidence, or rather testimony, in assurances of those who are in present enjoy-ment of it--if it is enjoyable. Whether this testimony has actually been given--and it is the only testimony worth a moment's consideration--is a disputed point Many persons while living this life have professed to have received it. But nobody profess-es, or ever has professed, to have received a communication of any kind from one in actual experience of the fore-life. "The souls as yet ungarmented," if such there are, are dumb to question. The Land beyond the Grave has been, if not observed, yet often and variously described: if not explored and surveyed, yet carefully charted. From among so many accounts of it that we have, he must be fastidious indeed who can not be suited. But of the Fatherland that spreads before the cradle--the great Heretofore, wherein we all dwelt if we are to dwell in the Hereafter, we have no account. Nobody professes knowledge of that. No testimony reaches our ears of flesh concerning its topographical or other features; no one has been so enterprising as to wrest from its actual inhabitants any particulars of their character and appearance, to refresh our memory withal. And among educated experts and professional proponents of worlds to be there is a general denial of its existence.

I am of their way of thinking about that. The fact that we have no recollection of a former life is entirely conclusive of the matter. To have lived an unrecollected life is impossible and unthinkable, for there would be nothing to connect the new life with the old--no thread of continuity--nothing that persisted from the one life to the other. The later birth is that of another person, an altogether different being, unrelated to the first--a new John Smith succeeding to the late Tom Jones.

Let us not be misled here by a false analogy. Today I may get a thwack on the mazzard which will give me an intervening season of unconsciousness between yesterday and tomorrow. Thereafter I may live to a green old age with no recollection of anything that I knew, or did, or was before the accident; yet I shall be the same person, for between the old life and the new there will be a ***nexus***, a thread of continuity, something spanning the gulf from the one state to the other, and the same in both--namely, my body with its habits, capacities and powers. That is I; that identifies me as my former self--authenticates and credentials me as the person that incurred the cranial mischance, dislodging memory.

But when death occurs ***all*** is dislodged if memory is; for between two merely mental or spiritual existences memory is the only ***nexus*** conceivable; consciousness of identity is the only identity. To live again without memory of having lived before is to live another. Re-existence without recollection is absurd; there is nothing to re-exist.

OPPORTUNITY

THIS is not a country of equal fortunes; outside a Socialist's dream no such country exists or can exist. But as nearly as possible this is a country of equal opportunities for those who begin life with nothing but nature's endowments--and of such is the kingdom of success.

In nine instances in ten successful Americans--that is Americans who have succeeded in any worthy ambition or legitimate field of endeavor--have started with nothing but the skin they stood in. It almost may be said, indeed, that to begin with nothing is a main condition of success--in America.

To a young man there is no such hopeless impediment as wealth or the expectation of wealth. Here a man and there a man will be born so abundantly endowed by nature as to overcome the handicap of artificial "advantages," but that is not the rule; usually the chap "born with a gold spoon in his mouth" puts in his time sucking that spoon, and without other employment. Counting possession of the spoon success, why should he bestir himself to achieve what he already has?

The real curled darling of opportunity has nothing in his mouth but his teeth and his appetite--he knows, or is likely to know, what it is to feel his belly sticking to his back. If he have brains a-plenty he will get on, for he must be up and doing--the penalty of indiligence is famine. If he have not, he may up and do to the uttermost satisfaction of his mind and heart, but the end of that man is failure, with possibly Socialism, that last resort of conscious incompetence. It fatigues, this talk of the narrowing opportunities of today, the "closed avenues to success," and the rest of it. Doubtless it serves its purpose of making mischief for the tyrant trusts and the wicked rich generally, but in a six months' bound volume of it there is not enough of truth to float a religion.

Men of brains never had a better chance than now to accomplish all that it is desirable that they should accomplish; and men of no brains never did have much of a chance, nor under any possible conditions can have in this country, nor in any other. They are nature's failures, God's botchwork. Let us be sorry for them, treating them justly and generously; but the Socialism that would level us all down to their plane of achievement and reward is a proposal of which they are themselves the only proponents.

Opportunity, indeed! Who is holding me from composing a great opera that would make me rich and famous?

What oppressive laws forbade me to work my passage up the Yukon as deckhand on a steamboat and discover the gold along Bonanza creek?

What is there in our industrial system that conceals from me the secret of making diamonds from charcoal?

Why was it not I who, entering a lawyer's office as a suitable person to sweep it out, left it as an appointed Justice of the Supreme Court?

The number of actual and possible sources of profit and methods of distinction is infinite. Not all the trusts in the world combined in one trust of trusts could appreciably reduce it--could condemn to permanent failure one man with the talent and the will to succeed. They can abolish that doubtful benefactor of the "small dealer," who lives by charging too much, and that very thickly disguised blessing the "drummer," whom they have to add to the price of everything they sell; but for every opportunity they close they open a new one and leave untouched a thousand actual and a million possible ones. As to their dishonest practices, these are conspicuous and striking, because "lumped," but no worse than the silent, steady aggregate of cheating; by which their constituent firms and individuals, formerly consumed the consumer without his special wonder.

CHARITY

THE promoter of organized charity protests against "the wasteful and mischievous method of undirected relief." He means, naturally, relief that is not directed by somebody else than the person giving it--undirected by him and his kind--professional almoners--philanthropists who deem it more blessed to allot than to bestow. Indubitably much is wasted and some mischief done by indiscriminate giving--and individual givers are addicted to that faulty practice. But there is something to be said for "undirected relief" quite the same. It blesses not only him who receives (when he is worthy; and when he is not upon his own head be it), but him who gives. To those uncalculating persons who, despite the protests of the organized charitable, concede a certain moral value to the spontaneous impulses of the heart and read in the word "relief" a double meaning, the office of the mere distributor is imperfectly sacred. He is even without scriptural authority, and lives in the perpetual challenge of a moral *quo warranto*. Nevertheless he is not without his uses. He is a tapper of tills that do not open automatically. He is almoner to the uncompassionate, who but for him would give no alms. He negotiates unnatural but not censurable relations between selfishness and ingratitude. The good that he does is purely material. He makes two leaves of fat to grow where but one grew before, lessens the sum of gastric pangs and dorsal chills. All this is something, certainly, but it generates no warm and elevated sentiments and does nothing in mitigation of the poor's animosity to the rich. Organized charity is a sapid and savorless thing; its place among moral agencies is no higher than that of root beer.

Christ did not say "Sell whatsoever thou hast and give to the church to give to the poor." He did not mention the Associated Charities of the period. I do not find the words "The Little Sisters of the Poor ye have always with you," nor "Inasmuch as ye have done it unto the least of these Dorcas societies ye have done it unto me." Nowhere do I find myself commanded to enable others to comfort the afflicted and visit the sick and those in prison. Nowhere is recorded God's blessing upon him who makes himself a part of a charity machine--no, not even if he be the guiding lever of the whole mechanism.

Organized charity is a delusion and a snare. It enables Munniglut to think himself a good man for paying annual dues and buying transferable meal tickets. Munniglut is not thereby, a good man. On the Last Great Day, when he cowers in the Ineffable Presence and is asked for an accounting it will not help him to say, "Hearing that A was in want I gave money for his need to B." Nor will it help B to say, "When A was in distress I asked C to relieve him, and myself allotted the relief according to a resolution of D, E and F."

There are blessings and benefactions that one would willingly forego--among them the poor. Quack remedies for poverty amuse; a real specific would kindle a noble enthusiasm. Yet the world would lose much by it; human nature would suffer a change for the worse. Happily and unhappily poverty is not abolishable: "The poor ye have always with you" is a sentence that can never become unintelligible. Effect of a thousand causes, poverty is invincible, eternal. And since we must have it let us thank God for it and avail ourselves of all its advantages to mind and character. He who is not good to the deserving poor--who knows not those of his immediate environment, who goes not among them making inquiry of their personal needs, who does not wish with all his heart and both his hands to relieve them--is a fool.

EMANCIPATED WOMAN

WHAT I should like to know is, how "the enlargement of woman's sphere" by entrance into the various activities of commercial, professional and industrial life benefits the sex. It may please Helen Gougar and satisfy her sense of logical accuracy to say, as she does: "We women must work in order to fill the places left vacant by liquor-drinking men." But who filled these places before? Did they remain vacant, or were there then disappointed applicants, as now? If my memory serves, there has been no time in the period that it covers when the supply of workers--abstemious male workers--was not in excess of the demand. That it has always been so is sufficiently attested by the universally inadequate wage rate.

Employers seldom fail, and never for long, to get all the workmen they need. The field, then, into which women have put their sickles was already overcrowded with reapers. Whatever employment women have obtained has been got by displacing men--who would otherwise be supporting women. Where is the general advantage? We may shout "high tariff," "combination of capital," "demonetization of silver," and what not, but if searching for the cause of augmented poverty and crime, "industrial discontent," and the tramp evil, instead of dogmatically expounding it, we should take some account of this enormous, sudden addition to the number of workers seeking work. If any one thinks that within the brief period of a generation the visible supply of labor can be enormously augmented without profoundly affecting the stability of things and disastrously touching the interests of wage-workers, let no rude voice dispel his dream of such maleficent agencies as his slumbrous understanding may joy to affirm. And let our Widows of Ashur unlung themselves in advocacy of quack remedies for evils for which they themselves are cause; it remains true that when the contention of two lions for one bone is exacerbated by the accession of a lioness the squabble is not composable by stirring up some bears in the cage adjacent.

Indubitably a woman is under no obligation to sacrifice herself to the good of her sex by refusing needed employment in the hope that it may fall to a man gifted with dependent women. Nevertheless our congratulations are more intelligent when bestowed upon her individual head than when sifted into the hair of all Eve's daughters. This is a world of complexities, in which the lines of interest are so intertangled as frequently to transgress that of sex; and one ambitious to help but half the race may profitably know that every effort to that end provokes a counterbalancing mischief. The "enlargement of woman's opportunities" has benefited individual women. It has not benefited the sex as a whole, and has distinctly damaged the race. The mind that can not discern a score of great and irreparable general evils distinctly traceable to "emancipation of woman" is as impregnable to the light as a toad in a rock.

A marked demerit of the new order of things--the regime of female commercial service--is that its main advantage accrues, not to the race, not to the sex, not to the class, not to the individual woman, but to the person of least need and worth--the male employer. (Female employers in any considerable number there will not be, but those that we have could give the male ones profitable instruction in grinding the faces of their employees.) This constant increase of the army of labor--always and everywhere too large for the work in sight--by accession of a new contingent of natural oppressibles makes the very teeth of old Munniglut thrill with a poignant delight. It brings in that situation known as two laborers seeking one job---and one of them a person whose bones he can easily grind to make his bread. And Munniglut is a miller of skill and experience, dusted all over with the evidence of his useful craft. When Heaven has assisted the Daughters of Hope to open to women a new "avenue of opportunities" the first to enter and walk therein, like God in the Garden of Eden, is the good Mr. Munniglut, contentedly smoothing the folds out of the superior slope of his paunch, exuding the peculiar aroma of his oleagmous personality, and larding the new roadway with the overflow of a righteousness secreted by some spiritual gland stimulated to action by relish of his own identity. And ever thereafter the subtle suggestion of a fat Philistinism lingers along the path of progress like an assertion of a possessory right.

It is God's own crystal truth that in dealing with women unfortunate enough to be compelled to earn their own living and fortunate enough to have wrested from Fate an opportunity to do so, men of business and affairs treat them with about the same delicate consideration that they show to dogs and horses of the inferior breeds. It does not commonly occur to the wealthy "professional man," or "prominent merchant," to be ashamed to add to his yearly thousands a part of the salary justly due to his female bookkeeper or typewriter, who sits before him all day with an empty belly in order to have an habilimented back. He has a vague, hazy notion that the law of supply and demand is mandatory, and that in submitting himself to it by paying her a half of what he would have to pay a man of inferior efficiency he is supplying the world with a noble example of obedience. I must take the liberty to remind him that the law of supply and demand is not imperative; it is not a statute, but a phenomenon. He may reply: "It is imperative; the penalty for disobedience is failure. If I pay more in salaries and wages than I need to, my competitor will not; and with that advantage he will drive me from the field." If his margin of profit is so small that he must eke it out by coining the sweat of his workmen into nickels, I've nothing to say to him. Let him adopt in peace the motto, "I cheat to eat" I do not know why he should eat, but Nature, who has provided sustenance for the worming sparrow, the sparrowing owl, and the owling eagle, approves the needy man of prey, and makes a place for him at table.

Human nature is pretty well balanced; for every lacking virtue there is a rough substitute that will serve at a pinch--as cunning is the wisdom of the unwise, and ferocity the courage of the coward. Nobody is altogether bad; the scoundrel who has grown rich by underpaying the workmen in his factory will sometimes endow an asylum for indigent seamen. To oppress one's own workmen, and provide for the workmen of a neighbor--to skin those in charge of one's own interests, while cottoning and oiling the residuary product of another's skinnery--that is not very good benevolence, nor very good sense, but it serves in place of both. The man who eats **pate de fois gras** in the sweat of his girl cashier's face, or wears purple and fine linen in order that his typewriter may have an eocene gown and a pliocene hat, seems a tolerably satisfactory specimen of the genus thief; but let us not forget that in his own home--a fairly good one--he may enjoy and merit that highest and most honorable title in the hierarchy of woman's favor, "a good provider." One having a just claim to that glittering distinction should enjoy a sacred immunity from the coarse and troublesome question, "From whose backs and bellies do you provide?"

So much for the material results to the sex. What are the moral results? One does not like to speak of them, particularly to those who do not and can not know--to good women in whose innocent minds female immorality is inseparable from flashy gowning and the painted face; to foolish, book-taught men who honestly believe in some protective sanctity that hedges womanhood. If men of the world with years enough to have lived out of the old *regime* into the new would testify in this matter there would ensue a great rattling of dry bones in bodices of reform ladies. Nay, if the young man about town, knowing nothing of how things were in the "dark backward and abysm of time," but something of the moral difference between even so free-running a creature as the society girl and the average working girl of the factory, the shop and the office, would speak out (under assurance of immunity from prosecution) his testimony would be a surprise to the cartilaginous virgins, blowsy matrons, acrid relicts and hairy males of Emancipation. It would pain, too, some very worthy but unobservant persons not in sympathy with "the cause."

Certain significant facts are within the purview of all but the very young and the comfortably blind. To the woman of today the man of today is imperfectly polite. In place of reverence he gives her "deference;" to the language of compliment has succeeded the language of raillery. Men have almost forgotten how to bow. Doubtless the advanced female prefers the new manner, as may some of her less forward sisters, thinking it more sincere. It is not; our giddy grandfather talked high-flown nonsense because his heart had tangled his tongue. He treated his woman more civilly than we ours because he loved her better. He never had seen her on the "rostrum" and in the lobby, never had seen her in advocacy of herself, never had read her confessions of his sins, never had felt the stress of her competition, nor himself assisted by daily personal contact in rubbing the bloom off her. He did not know that her virtues were due to her secluded life, but thought, dear old boy, that they were a gift of God.

THE OPPOSING SEX

EMANCIPATION of woman is not of American invention. The "movement," like most others that are truly momentous, originated in Europe, and has broken through and broken down more formidable barriers of law, custom and tradition there than here. It is not true that the English married woman is "virtually a bond-woman" to her husband; that "she can hardly go and come without his consent, and usually he does not consent;" that "all she has is his." If there is such a thing as "the bitterness of the English married woman to the law," underlying it there is such a thing as ignorance of what the law is. The "subjection of woman," as it exists today in England, is customary and traditionary--a social, not a legal, subjection. Nowhere has law so sharply challenged that male dominion whose seat is in the harder muscles, the larger brain and the coarser heart And the law, it may be worth while to point out, was not of woman born; nor was it handed down out of Heaven engraved on tables of stone. Learned English judges have decided that virtually the term "marital rights" has no longer a legal signification. As one writer puts it, "The law has relaxed the husband's control over his wife's person and fortune, bit by bit, until legally it has left him nothing but the power to prevent her, if he is so disposed, and arrives in time, from jumping out of the window." He will find it greatly to his interest to arrive in time when he conveniently can, and to be so disposed, for the husband is still liable for the wife's torts; and if she makes the leap he may have to pay for the telescoping of a subjacent hat or two.

In England it is the Tyrant Man himself who is chafing in his chain. Not only is a husband still liable for the wrongs committed by the wife whom he has no longer the power to restrain from committing them, but in many ways--in one very important way--his obligation to her remains intact after she has had the self-sacrifice to surrender all obligation to him. Moreover, if his wife has a separate estate he has to endure the pain of seeing it hedged about from her creditors (themselves not altogether happy in the contemplation) with restrictions which do not hamper the right of recourse against his own. Doubtless all this is not without a softening effect upon his character, smoothing down his dispositional asperities and endowing him day by day with fresh accretions of humility. And that is good for him. I do not say that female autonomy is not among the most efficacious agencies for man's reclamation from the sin of pride; I only say that it is not indigenous to this country, the sweet, sweet home of the assassiness, the happy hunting ground of the whiplady, the paradise of the vitrioleuse.

If the protagonists of woman suffrage are frank they are shallow; if wise, uncandid. Continually they affirm their conviction that political power in the hands of women will give us better government. To proof of that proposition they address all the powers that they have and marshal such facts as can be compelled to serve under their flag. They either think or profess to think that if they can show that women's votes will purify politics they will have proved their case. That is not true; whether they know it or not, the strongest objection to woman suffrage would remain untouched. Pure politics is desirable, certainly, but it is not the chief concern of the best and most intelligent citizens. Good government is "devoutly to be wished," but more than good government we need good women. If all our public affairs were to be ordered with the goodness and wisdom of angels, and this state of perfection were obtained by sacrifice of any of those qualities which make the best of our women, if not what they should be, nor what the mindless male thinks them, at least what they are, we should have purchased the advantage too dearly. The effect of woman suffrage upon the country is of secondary importance: the question for profitable consideration is, How will it affect the character of woman? He who does not see in the goodness and charm of such women as are good and charming something incalculably more precious than any degree of political purity or national prosperity may be a patriot: doubtless he is; but also he has the distinction to be a pig.

I should like to ask the gallant gentlemen who vote for removal of woman's political disability if they have observed in the minds and manners of the women in the forefront of the movement nothing "ominous and drear." Are not these women different--I don't say worse, just different--from the best types of women of peace who are not exhibits and audibles? If they are different, is the difference of such a nature as to encourage a hope that activity in public affairs will work an improvement in women generally? Is "the glare of publicity" good for her growth in grace and winsomeness? Would a sane and sensible husband or lover willingly forego in wife or sweetheart all that the colonels of her sex appear to lack, or find in her all that they appear to have and to value?

A few more questions--addressed more particularly to veteran observers than to those to whom the world is new and strange. Have you observed any alteration in the manner of men toward women? If so, is it in the direction of greater rudeness or of more ceremonious respect? And again, if so, has not the change, in point of time, been coincident with the genesis and development of woman's "emancipation" and her triumphal entry into the field of "affairs"? Are you really desirous that the change go further? Or do you think that when women are armed with the ballot they will compel a return of the old *regime* of deference and delicate consideration--extorting by their power the tribute once voluntarily paid to their weakness? Is there any known way by which women can at once be our political equals and our social superiors, our competitors in the sharp and bitter struggle for glory, gain or bread, and the objects of our unselfish and undiminished devotion? The present predicts the future; of the foreshadow of the coming event all sensitive female hearts feel the chill. For whatever advantages, real or illusory, some women enjoy under this *regime* of partial "emancipation" all women pay. Of the coin in which payment is made the shouldering shouters of the sex have not a groat and can bear the situation with impunity. They have either passed the age of masculine attention or were born without the means to its accroachment. Dwelling in the open bog, they can afford to defy eviction.

While men did nearly all the writing and public speaking of the world, setting so the fashion in thought, women, naturally extolled with true sexual extravagance, came to be considered, even by themselves, as a very superior order of beings, with something in them of divinity which was denied to man. Not only were they represented as better, generally, than men, as indeed anybody could see that they were, but their goodness was supposed to be a kind of spiritual endowment and more or less independent of environmental influences.

We are changing all that. Women are beginning to do much of the writing and public speaking, and not only are they going to extol us (to the fattening of our conceit) but they are bound to disclose, even to the unthinking, certain defects of character in themselves which their silence had veiled. Their competition, too, in several kinds of affairs will slowly but certainly provoke resentment, and moreover expose them to temptations which will distinctly lower the morality of their sex. All these changes, and many more having a similar effect and significance, are occurring with amazing rapidity, and the stated results are already visible to even the blindest observation. In accurate depiction of the new order of things conjecture fails, but so much we know: the woman-superstition has already received its death wound and must soon expire.

Everywhere, and in no reverential spirit, men are questioning the dear old idolatry; not "sapping a solemn creed with solemn sneer," but dispassionately applying to its basic doctrine the methods of scientific criticism. He who within even the last twenty years has not marked in society, in letters, in art, in everything, a distinct change in man's attitude toward women--a change which, were one a woman, one would not wish to see--may reasonably conclude that much, otherwise observable, is hidden by his nose. In the various movements--none of them consciously iconoclastic--engaged in overthrowing this oddest of modern superstitions there is something to deprecate, and even deplore, but the superstition can be spared. It never had much in it that was either creditable or profitable, and all through its rituals ran a note of insincerity which was partly Nature's protest against the rites, but partly, too, hypocrisy. There is no danger that good men will ever cease to respect and love good women, and if bad men ever cease to adore them for their sex when not beating them for their virtues the gain in consistency will partly offset the loss in religious ecstasy.

Let the patriot abandon his fear, his betters their hope, that only the low class woman will vote--the unlettered wench of the slums, the raddled hag of the dives, the war-painted *protegee* of the police. Into the vortex of politics goes every floating thing that is free to move. The summons to the polls will be imperative and incessant. Duty will thunder it from every platform, conscience whisper it into every ear, pride, interest, the lust of victory--all the motives that impel men to partisan activity will act with equal power upon women as upon men; and to all the other forces flowing irresistibly toward the polls will be added the suasion of men themselves. The price of votes will not decline because of the increased supply, although it will in most instances be offered in currencies too subtle to be counted. As now, the honest and respectable elector will habitually take bribes in the invisible coin of the realm of Sentiment--a mintage peculiarly valued by woman. For one reason or another all women will vote, even those who now view the "right" widi aversion. The observer who has marked the strength and activity of the forces pent in the dark drink of politics and given off in the act of bibation will not expect inaction to the victim of the "habit," be he male or she female. In the partisan, conviction is compulsion---opinions bear fruit in conduct. The partisan thinks in deeds, and woman is by nature a partisan--a blessing for which the Lord has never made her male relatives and friends sufficiently thankful. Not a mere man of them would have the effrontery to ask her toleration if she were not Depend upon it, the full strength of the female vote will eventually be cast at every election. And it would be well indeed for civilization and the interests of the race if woman suffrage meant no more than going to the polling-place and polling--which clearly is all that it has been thought out to mean by the headless horsemen spurring their new hobbies bravely at the tail of the procession. That would be a very simple matter; the opposition based upon the impropriety of the female rubbing shoulders at the polls with such scurvy blackguards as ourselves may with advantage be retired from service. Nor is it particularly important what men and measures the women will vote for. By one means or another Tyrant Man will have his way; the Opposing Sex can merely obstruct him in his way of having it. And should that obstruction ever be too pronounced, the party line and the sex line coinciding, woman suffrage will then and henceforth be no more.

In the politics of this bad world majorities are of several kinds. One of the most "overwhelming" is made up of these simple elements: (1) a numerical minority; (2) a military superiority. If not a single election were ever in any degree affected by it, the introduction of woman suffrage into our scheme of manners and morals would nevertheless be the most momentous and mischievous event of modern history. Compared with the action of this destructive solvent, that of all other disintegrating agencies concerned in our decivilization is as the languorous indiligence of rosewater to the mordant fury of nitric acid.

Lively Woman is indeed, as Carlyle would put it, "hellbent" on purification of politics by adding herself as an ingredient. It is unlikely that the injection of her personality into the contention (and politics is essentially a contention) will allay any animosities, sweeten any tempers, elevate any motives. The strifes of women are distinctly meaner than those of men--which are out of all reason mean; their

methods of overcoming opponents distinctly more unscrupulous. That their participation in politics will notably alter the conditions of the game is not to be denied;
that, unfortunately, is obvious; but that it will make the player less malignant and
the playing more honorable is a proposition in support of which one can utter a deal
of gorgeous nonsense, with a less insupportable sense of its unfitness, than in the
service of any other delusion.

The frosty truth is that except in the home the influence of women is not elevating, but debasing. When they stoop to uplift men who need uplifting, they are
themselves pulled down, and that is all that is accomplished. Wherever they come
into familiar contact with men who are not their relatives they impart nothing,
they receive all; they do not affect us with their notions of morality; we infect them
with ours.

In the last forty years, in this country, they have entered a hundred avenues
of activity from which they were previously debarred by an unwritten law. They
are found in the offices, the shops, the factories. Like Charles Lamb's fugitive pigs,
they have run up all manner of streets. Does any one think that in that time there
has been an advance in professional, commercial and industrial morality? Are lawyers more scrupulous, tradesmen more honest? When one has been served by a
"saleslady" does one leave the shop with a feebler sense of injury than was formerly
inspired by a transaction at the counter--a duller consciousness of being oneself the
commodity that has changed hands? Have actresses elevated the stage to a moral
altitude congenial to the colder virtues? In studios of the artists is the "sound of
revelry by night" invariably a deep, masculine bass? In literature are the immoral
books--the books "dealing" with questionable "questions"--always, or even commonly, written by men?

There is one direction in which "emancipation of woman" and enlargement
of her "sphere" have wrought a reform: they have elevated the ***personnel*** of the
little dinner party in the "private room." Formerly, as any veteran man-about-town
can testify, if he will, the female contingent of the party was composed of persons
altogether unspeakable. That element now remains upon its reservation; among
the superior advantages enjoyed by the man-about-town of today is that of the
companionship, at his dinner *in camera*, of ladies having an honorable vocation.
In the corridors of the "French restaurant" the swish of Pseudonyma's skirt is no

longer heard; she has been superseded by the Princess Tap-tap (with Truckle & Cinch), by my lady Snip-snip (from the "emporium" of Boltwhack & Co.), by Miss Chink-chink, who sits at the receipt of customs in that severely un-French restaurant, the Maison Hash. That the man-about-town has been morally elevated by this Emancipation of Girl from the seclusion of home to that of the "private room" is too obvious for denial. Nothing so uplifts Tyrant Man as the table talk of good young women who earn their own living.

I do not wish to be altogether ironical about this rather serious matter--not so much so as to forfeit anything of lucidity. Let me state, then, in all earnestness and sobriety and simplicity of speech, what is known to every worldly-wise male dweller in the cities, to every scamp and scapegrace of the clubs, to every reformed sentimentalist and every observer with a straight eye--namely, that in all the various classes of young women in our cities who support, or partly support, themselves in vocations which bring them into personal contact with men, female chastity is a vanishing tradition. In the lives of the "main and general" of these, all those *considerate* which have their origin in personal purity, and cluster about it, and are its signs and safeguards, have almost ceased to cut a figure. It is needless to remind me that there are exceptions--I know that. With some of them I have personal acquaintance, or think I have, and for them a respect withheld from any woman of the rostrum who points to their misfortune and calls it emancipation--to their need and calls it a spirit of independence. It is not from these good girls that you will hear the flippant boast of an unfettered life, with "freedom to develop;" nor is it they who will be foremost and furious in denial and resentment of my statements regarding the morals of their class. They do not know the whole truth, thank Heaven, but they know enough for a deprecation too deep to find relief in a cheap affirmation of woman's purity, which is, and always has been, the creature of seclusion.

The fitness of women for political activity is not in present question; I am considering the fitness of political activity for women. For women as men say they are, wish them to be, and try to think them, it is unfit altogether--as unfit as anything else that "mixes them up" with us, compelling a communication and association that are not social. If we wish to have women who are different from ourselves in knowledge, character, accomplishments, manners; as different mentally as physically--and in these and in all odier expressible differences reside all the charms that they have for us--we must keep them, or they must keep themselves, in an environment unlike our own. One would think that obvious to the meanest capacity, and might even hope that it would be understood by the Daughters of Thunder. Possibly the Advanced One, hospitably accepting her karma, is not concerned to be charming to "the likes o' we'"--would prefer the companionship of her blue gingham umbrella, her corkscrew curls, her epicene audiences and her name in the newspapers. Perhaps she is content with the comfort of her raucous voice. Therein she is unwise, for self-interest is the first law. When we no longer find woman charming we may find a way to make them more useful--more truly useful, even, than the speech-ladies would have them make themselves by competition. Really, there is nothing in the world between them and slavery but their power of interesting us; and that has its origin in the very differences which the Colonels are striving to abolish. God has made no law of miracles and none of His laws are going to be suspended in deference to woman's desire to achieve familiarity without contempt. If she wants to please she must retain some scrap of novelty; if she desires our respect she must not be always in evidence, disclosing the baser side of her character, as in competition with us she must do (as we do to one another) or lamentably fail. Mrs. Edmund Gosse, like "Ouida," Mrs. Atherton, and all other women of brains, declares that the taking of unfair advantages--the lack of magnanimity--is a leading characteristic of her sex. Mrs. Gosse adds, with reference to men's passive acquiescence in this monstrous folly of "emancipation," that possibly our quiet may be the calm before the storm; and she utters this warning, which, also, more strongly, "Ouida" has uttered: "How would it be with us if the men should suddenly rise *en masse* and throw the whole surging lot of us into convents and harems?"

It is not likely that men will "rise *en masse*" to undo the mischief wrought by noisy protagonists of Woman Suffrage working like beavers to rear their airy fad upon the sandy foundation of masculine tolerance and inattention. No rising will be needed. All that is required for the wreck of their hopes is for a wave of reason to slide a little farther up the sands of time, "loll out its large tongue, lick the whole labor flat" The work has prospered so far only because nobody but its promoters has taken it seriously. It has not engaged attention from those having the knowledge and the insight to discern beneath its cap-and-bells and the motley that is its only wear a serious menace to all that civilized men hold precious in woman. It is of the nature of men--themselves cheerful polygamists, with no penitent intentions--to set a high value upon chastity in woman. (We need not inquire why they do so; those to whom the reasons are not clear can profitably remain in the valley of the shadow of ignorance.) Valuing it, they purpose having it, or some considerable numerical presumption of it. As they perceive that in a general way women are virtuous in proportion to the remoteness of their lives and interests from the lives and interests of men--their seclusion from the influences of which men's own vices are a main part--an easy and peaceful means will doubtless be found for the repression of the shouters.

In the orchestration of mind woman's instruments might have kept silence without injury to the volume and quality of the music; efface the impress of her touch upon the world and, by those who come after, the blank must be diligently sought. Go to the top of any large city and look about and below. It is not much that you will see, but it represents an amazing advance from the conditions of primitive man. No where in the wide survey will you see the work of woman. It is all the work of men's hands, and before it was wrought into form and substance, existed as conscious creations in men's brains. Concealed within the visible forms of buildings and ships--themselves miracles of thought--lie such wonder-worlds of invention and discovery as no human life is long enough to explore, no human understanding capacious enough to hold in knowledge. If, like Asmodeus, we could rive the roofs and see woman's part of this prodigious exhibition--the things that she has actually created with her brain--what kind of display would it be? It is probable that all the intellectual energy expended by women from first to last would not have sufficed, if directed into the one channel, for the genesis and evolution of the modern bicycle.

I once heard a lady who had playfully competed with men in a jumping match gravely attribute her defeat to the trammeling of her skirt. Similarly, women are pleased to explain their penury of mental achievement by repressive education and custom, and therein they are not altogether in heresy. But even in regions where they have ever had the freedom of the quarries they have not builded themselves monuments. Nobody, for example, is holding them from greatness in poetry, which needs no special education, and music, in which they have always been specially educated; yet where is the great poem by a woman? where the great musical composition? In the grammar of literature what is the feminine of Homer, of Shaks-pere, of Goethe, of Hugo? What female names are the equivalents of the names of Beethoven, Mozart, Chopin, Wagner? Women are not musicians--they "sing and play." In short, if woman had no better claim to respect and affection than her brain; no sweeter charms than those of her reason; no means of suasion but her power upon men's convictions, she would long ago have been "improved off the face of the earth." As she is, men accord her such homage as is compatible with contempt, such immunities as are consistent with exaction; but whereas she is not altogether filled with light and is moreover, imperfectly reverent, it is but right that in obedience to Scriptural injunction she keep silence in our churches while we are worshipping Ourselves.

She will not have it so, the good, good girl; as moral as the best of us, she will be as intellectual as the rest of us. She will have out her little taper and set the rivers of thought all ablaze, legging it over the land from stream to stream till all are fired. She will widen her sphere, forsooth, herself no wider than before. It is not enough that we have edified her a pedestal and perform impossible rites in celebration of her altitude and distinction. It does not suffice that with never a smile we assure her that she is the superior sex--a whopper by the repetition whereof certain callow youth among us have incurred the divine vengeance of belief. It does not satisfy her that she is indubitably gifted with pulchritude and an unquestionable genius for its embellishing; that Nature has endowed her with a prodigious knack at accroach-ment, whereby the male of her species is lured to a suitable doom. No; she has taken unto herself in these evil days that "intelligent discontent" which giveth its beloved fits. To her flock of graces and virtues she must add our one poor ewe lamb of brains. Well, I tell her that intellect is a monster which devours beauty; that the woman of exceptional mind is exceptionally masculine in face, figure, action; that in trans-planting brains to an unfamiliar soil God leaves much of the original earth about the roots. And so with a reluctant farewell to Lovely Woman, I humbly withdraw from her presence and hasten to overtake the receding periphery of her "sphere."

One moment more. Mesdames: I crave leave to estop your disfavor--which were affliction and calamity--by "defining my position" in the words of one of yourselves, who has said of me (though with reprehensible exaggeration, believe me) that I hate woman and love women--have an acute animosity to your sex and adoring each individual member of it. What matters my opinion of your under-standings so long as I am in bondage to your charms? Moreover, there is one service of incomparable utility and dignity for which I esteem you eminently fit--to be mothers of men.

THE AMERICAN SYCOPHANT

AN AMERICAN newspaper holds this opinion: "If republican government had done nothing else than give independence to American character and preserve it from the servility inseparable from the allegiance to kings, it would have accom-plished a great work."

I do not doubt that the writer of that sentence believes that republican govern-ment has actually wrought the change in human nature which challenges his admi-ration. He is very sure that his countrymen are not sycophants; that before rank and power and wealth they stand covered, maintaining "the godlike attitude of freedom and a man" and exulting in it. It is not true; it is an immeasurable distance from the truth. We are as abject toadies as any people on earth--more so than any European people of similar civilization. When a foreign emperor, king, prince or nobleman comes among us the rites of servility that we execute in his honor are baser than any that he ever saw in his own land. When a foreign nobleman's prow puts into shore the American shin is pickled in brine to welcome him; and if he come not in adequate quantity those of us who can afford the expense go swarming over sea to struggle for front places in his attention. In this blind and brutal scramble for social recognition in Europe the traveling American toady and impostor has many chances of success: he is commonly unknown even to ministers and consuls of his own country, and these complaisant gentlemen, rather than incur the risk of erring on the wrong side, take him at his own valuation and push him in where his obscu-rity being again in his favor, he is treated with kindly toleration, and sometimes a genuine hospitality, to which he has no shadow of right nor title, and which, if he were a gentleman, he would not accept if it were voluntarily proffered. It should be said in mitigation that all this delirious abasement in no degree tempers his rancor against the system of which the foreign notable is the flower and fruit. He keeps his servility sweet by preserving it in the salt of vilification. In the character of a blatant blackguard the American snob is so happily disguised that he does not know himself.

An American newspaper once printed a portrait of her whom the irreverent Briton had a reprehensible habit of designating colloquially as "The Old Lady," But the editor in question did not so designate her--his simple American manhood and republican spirit would not admit that she was a lady. So he contented himself with labeling the portrait "Her Most Gracious Majesty, Queen Victoria" This incident raises an important question.

Important Question Raised by This Incident: Is it better to be a subject and a man, or a citizen and a flunkey--to own the sway of a "gory tyrant" and retain one's self-respect, or dwell, a "sovereign elector," in the land of liberty and disgrace it?

However it may be customary for English newspapers to designate the English sovereign, they are at least not addicted to sycophancy in designating the rulers of other countries than their own. They would not say "His Abracadabral Humpti-dumptiness Emperor William," nor "His Pestilency the Speaker of the American House of Representatives." They would not think of calling even the most ornately self-bemedaled American sovereign elector "His Badgesty." Of a foreign nobleman they do not say "His Lordship;" they will not admit that he is a lord; nor when speaking of their own noblemen do they spell "lord" with a capital L, as we do. In brief, when mentioning foreign dignitaries, of whatever rank in their own coun-tries, the English press is simply and serviceably descriptive: the king is a king, the queen a queen, the jack a jack. We use "another kind of common sense." At the very foundation of our political system lies the denial of hereditary and artificial rank. Our fathers created this government as a protest against all that, and all that it implies. They virtually declared that kings and noblemen could not breathe here, and no American loyal to the principles of the Revolution which made him one will ever say in his own country "Your Majesty" or "Your Lordship"--the words would choke him and they ought.

There are a few of us who keep the faith, who do not bow the knee to Baal, who hold fast to what is high and good in the doctrine of political equality; in whose hearts the altar-fires of rational liberty are kept aglow, beaconing the darkness of that illimitable inane where their countrymen, inaccessible to the light, wander witless in the bogs of political unreason, alternately adoring and damning the man-made gods of their own stature. Of that bright band fueling the bale-fires of political consistency I can not profess myself a member in good standing. In view of this general recreancy and treason to the principles that our fathers established by the sword--having in constant observation this almost universal hospitality to the solemn nonsense of hereditary rank and unearned distinction, my faith in practical realization of republican ideals is small, and I falter in the work of their maintenance in the interest of a people for whom they are too good. Seeing that we are immune to none of the evils besetting monarchies, excepting those for which we secretly yearn; that inequality of fortune and unjust allotment of honors are as conspicuous among us as elsewhere; that the tyranny of individuals is as intolerable, and that of the public more so; that the law's majesty is a dream and its failure a fact--hearing everywhere the footfalls of disorder and the watchwords of anarchy, I despair of the republic and catch in every breeze that blows "a cry prophetic of its fall."

I have seen a vast crowd of Americans change color like a field of waving grain, as it uncovered to do such base homage to a petty foreign princess as in her own country she had never received. I have seen full-grown, self-respecting American citizens tremble and go speechless when spoken to by the Emperor of Brazil. I have seen a half-dozen American gentlemen in evening clothes trying to outdo one another in the profundity of their bows in the presence of the nigger King of Hawaii. I have not seen a Chinese "Earl" borne in a chair by four Americans officially detailed for the disgraceful service, but it was done, and did not evoke a hiss of disapproval. And I did not--thank Heaven!--observe the mob of American "simple republicans" that dogged the heels of a disreputable little Frenchman who is a count by courtesy only, and those of an English duke quietly attending to his business of making a living by being a married man. The republican New World is no less impested with servility than the monarchial Old. One form of government may be better than another for this purpose or for that; all are alike in the futility of their influence upon human character. None can affect man's instinctive abasement in the contemplation of power and rank.

Not only are we no less sycophantic than the people of monarchial countries; we are more so. We grovel before their exalted personages, and perform in addition a special prostration at the clay feet of our own idols--which *they* do not revere. The typical "subject," hat-in-hand to his sovereign and his nobleman, is a less shameful figure than the "citizen" executing his genuflexion before the public of which he is himself a part. No European court journal, no European courtier, was ever more abject in subservience to the sovereign than are the American newspaper and the American politician in flattery of the people. Between the courtier and the demagogue I see nothing to choose. They are moved by the same sentiment and fired by the same hope. Their method is flattery, and their purpose profit. Their adulation is not a testimony to character, but a tribute to power, or the shadow of power. If this country were governed by its criminal idiots we should have the same attestations of their goodness and wisdom, the same competition for their favor, the same solemn doctrine that their voice is the voice of God. Our children would be brought up to believe that an Idiotocracy is the only natural and rational form of government And for my part I'm not at all sure that it would not be a pretty good political system, as political systems go. I have always, however, cherished a secret faith in Smithocracy, which seems to combine the advantages of both the monarchial and the republican idea. If all the offices were held for life by Smiths--the senior John being President--we should have a settled and orderly succession to allay all fears of anarchy and a sufficiently wide eligibility to feed the fires of patriotic ambition. All could not be Smiths, but many could marry into the family.

The Harrison "progress" left its heritage of shame, whereof each abaser would gladly have washed the hands of him in his neighbor's basin. All this was in due order of Nature, and was to have been expected. It was a phenomenon of the same character as, in the loves of the low, the squabbling consequent upon satiety and shame. We could not slink out of sight; we could deny our sycophancy, albeit we might give it another name; but we could somewhat medicine our damaged self-esteem by dealing damnation 'round on one another. The blush of shame turned easily to the glow of indignation, and many a hot hatred was kindled at the rosy flame of self-contempt. Persons conscious of having dishonored themselves are doubly sensitive to any indignity put upon them by others. The vices and follies of human nature are interdependent; they do not move alone, nor are they singly aroused to activity. In my judgment, this entire incident of the President's "tour" was infinitely discreditable to President and people. I do not go into the question of his motive in making it. Be that what it may, the manner of it seems to me an outrage upon all the principles and sentiments underlying republican institutions. In all but the name it was a "royal progress"--the same costly ostentation, the same civic and military pomp, the same solemn and senseless adulation, the same abasement of spirit of the Many before the One. And according to republican traditions, ten thousand times a year affirmed, in every way in which affirmation is possible, we fondly persuade ourselves, as a true faith in the hearts of our hearts, that the One is the inferior of the Many! And it is no mere political catch-phrase: he *is* their servant; he *is* their creature; all that in him to which they grovel (dignifying and justifying their instinctive and inherited servility by names as false as anything in ceremonial imposture) they themselves have made, as truly as the heathen has made the wooden god before which he performs his unmanly rite. It is precisely this thing--the superiority of the people to their servants--that constitutes, and was by our fathers understood to constitute, the essential, fundamental difference between the monarchial system which they uprooted and the democratic one which they planted in its stead. Deluded men! how little they guessed the length and strength and vitality of the roots left in the soil of the centuries when their noxious harvestage of mischievous institutions had been cast as rubbish to the void!

I am no contestant for forms of government--no believer in either the practical value or the permanence of any that has yet been devised. That all men are created equal, in the best and highest sense of the phrase, I hold; not as I observe it held by others, but as a living faith. That an officeholder is a servant of the people; that I am his political superior, owing him no deference, and entitled to such deference from him as may be serviceable to keep him in mind of his subordination--these are propositions which command my assent, which I *feel* to be true and which determine the character of my personal relations with those whom they concern. That I should give my hand, or bend my neck, or uncover my head to any man in homage to or recognition of his office, great or small, is to me simply inconceivable. These tricks of servility with the softened names are the vestiges of an involuntary allegiance to power extraneous to the performer. They represent in our American life obedience and propitiation in their most primitive and odious forms. The man who speaks of them as manifestations of a proper respect for "the President's great office" is either a rogue, a dupe or a journalist They come to us out of a fascinating but terrible past as survivals of servitude. They speak a various language of oppression, and the superstition of man-worship; they cany forward the traditions of the sceptre and the lash. Through the plaudits of the people may be heard always the faint, far cry of the beaten slave.

Respect? Respect the good. Respect the wise. Respect the dead. Let the President look to it that he belongs to one of these classes. His going about the country in gorgeous state and barbaric splendor as the guest of a thieving corporation, but at our expense--shining and dining and swining--unsouling himself of clotted nonsense in pickled platitudes calculated for the meridian of Coon Hollow, Indiana, but ingeniously adapted to each water tank on the line of his absurd "progress," does not prove it, and the presumption of his "great office" is against him.

Can you not see, poor misguided "fellow citizens," how you permit your political taskmasters to forge leg-chains of your follies and load you down with them? Will nothing teach you that all this fuss-and-feathers, all this ceremony, all this official gorgeousness and brass-banding, this "manifestation of a proper respect for the nation's head" has no decent place in American life and American politics? Will no experience open your stupid eyes to the fact that these shows are but absurd imitations of royalty, to hold you silly while you are plundered by the managers of the performance?--that while you toss your greasy caps in air and sustain them by the ascending current of your senseless hurrahs the programmers are going through your blessed pockets and exploiting your holy dollars? No; you feel secure; "power is of the People," and you can effect a change of robbers every four years. Inestimable privilege--to pull off the glutted leech and attach the lean one! And you can not even choose among the lean leeches, but must accept those designated by the programmers and showmen who have the reptiles on tap! But then you are not "subjects;" you are "citizens"--there is much in that Your tyrant is not a "King;" he is a "President." He does not occupy a "throne," but a "chair." He does not succeed to it by inheritance; he is pitchforked into it by the boss. Altogether, you are distinctly better off than the Russian mujik who wears his shirt outside his trousers and has never shaken hands with the Czar in all his life.

I hold that kings and noblemen can not breathe in America. When they set foot upon our soil their kingship and their nobility fall away from them like the chains of a slave in England. Whatever a man may be in his own country, here he is but a man. My countrymen may do as they please, lickspittling the high and mighty of other nations even to the filling of their spiritual bellies, but I make a stand for simple American manhood. I will meet no man on this soil who expects from me a greater deference than I could properly accord to the President of my own country. My allegiance to republican institutions is slack through lack of faith in them as a practical system of governing men as men are. All the same, I will call no man "Your Majesty," nor "Your Lordship." For me to meet in my own country a king or a nobleman would require as much preliminary negotiation as an official interview between the Mufti of Moosh and the Ahkoond of Swat. The form of salutation and the style and tide of address would have to be settled definitively and with precision. With some of my most esteemed and patriotic friends the matter is more simple; their generosity in concession fills me with admiration and their forbearance in exaction challenges my astonishment as one of the seven wonders of American hospitality. In fancy I see the ceremony of their "presentation" and as examples of simple republican dignity I commend their posture to the youth of this fair New World, inviting particular attention to the grand, bold curves of character shown in the outlines of the Human Ham.

A DISSERTATION ON DOGS

OF ALL anachronisms and survivals, the love of the dog; is the most reasonless. Because, some thousands of years ago, when we wore other skins than our own and sat enthroned upon our haunches, tearing tangles of tendons from raw bones with our teeth, the dog ministered purveyorwise to our savage needs, we go on cherishing him to this day, when his only function is to lie sun-soaken on a door mat and insult us as we pass in and out, enamored of his fat superfluity. One dog in a thousand earns his bread--and takes beefsteak; the other nine hundred and ninety-nine we maintain, by cheating the poor, in the style suitable to their state.

The trouble with the modern dog is that he is the same old dog. Not an inch has the rascal advanced along the line of evolution. We have ceased to squat upon our naked haunches and gnaw raw bones, but this companion of the childhood of the race, this vestigial remnant of *juventus mundi* this dismal anachronism, this veteran inharmony of the scheme of things, the dog, has abated no jot nor tittle of his unthinkable objection-ableness since the morning stars sang together and he had sat up all night to deflate a lung at the performance. Possibly he may some time be improved otherwise than by effacement, but at present he is still in that early stage of reform that is not incompatible with a mouthful of reformer.

The dog is a detestable quadruped. He knows more ways to be unmentionable than can be suppressed in seven languages.

The word "dog" is a term of contempt the world over. Poets have sung and prosaists have prosed of the virtues of individual dogs, but nobody has had the hardihood to eulogize the species. No man loves the Dog; he loves his own dog or dogs, and there he stops; the force of perverted affection can no further go. He loves his own dog partly because that thrifty creature, ever cadging when not maurauding, tickles his vanity by fawning upon him as the visible source of steaks and bones; and partly because the graceless beast insults everybody else, harming as many as he dares. The dog is an encampment of fleas, and a reservoir of sinful smells. He is prone to bad manners as the sparks fly upward. He has no discrimination; his loyalty is given to the person that feeds him, be the same a blackguard or a murderer's mother. He fights for his master without regard to the justice of the quarrel--wherein he is no better than a patriot or a paid soldier. There are men who are proud of a dog's love--and dogs love that kind of men. There are men who, having the privilege of loving women, insult them by loving dogs; and there are women who forgive and respect their canine rivals. Women, I am told, are true cynolaters; they adore not only dogs, but Dog--not only their own horrible little beasts, but those of others. But women will love anything; they love men who love dogs. I sometimes wonder how it is that of all our women among whom the dog fad is prevalent none have incurred the husband fad, or the child fad. Possibly there are exceptions, but it seems to be a rule that the female heart which has a dog in it is without other lodgers. There is not, I suppose, a very wild and importunate demand for accommodation. For my part, I do not know which is the less desirable, the tenant or the tenement There are dogs that submit to be kissed by women base enough to kiss them; but they have a secret, coarse revenge. For the dog is a joker, withal, gifted with as much humor as is consistent with biting.

Miss Louise Imogen Guiney has replied to Mrs. Meynell's proposal to abolish the dog--a proposal which Miss Guiney has the originality to call "original." Divested of its "literature," Miss Guiney's plea for the defendant consists, essentially, of the following assertions: (1) Dogs are whatever their masters are. (2) They bite only those who fear them. (3) Really vicious dogs are not found nearer than Constantinople. (4) Only wronged dogs go mad, and hydrophobia is retaliation. (5) In actions for damages for dog-bites judicial prejudice is against the dog. (6) "Dogs are continually saving children from death." (7) Association with dogs begets piety, tenderness, mercy, loyalty, and so forth; in brief, the dog is an elevating influence: "to walk modestly at a dog's heels is a certificate of merit!" As to that last, if Miss Guiney had ever observed the dog himself walking modestly at the heels of another dog she would perhaps have wished that it was not the custom of her sex to seal the certificate of merit with a kiss.

In all this absurd woman's statements, thus fairly epitomized, there is not one that is true--not one of which the essential falsity is not evident, obvious, conspicuous to even the most delinquent observation. Yet with the smartness and smirk of a graduating seminary girl refuting Epicurus she marshals them against the awful truth that every year in Europe and the United States alone more than five thousand human beings the of hydrophobia--a fact which her controversial conscience does not permit her to mention. The names on this needless death-roll are mostly those of children, the sins of whose parents in cherishing their own hereditary love of dogs is visited upon their children because they have not the intelligence and agility to get out of the way. Or perhaps they lack that tranquil courage upon which Miss Guiney relies to avert the canine tooth from her own inedible shank.

Finally this amusing illogician, this type and example of the female controversialist, has the hardihood to hope that there may be fathers who can see their children the the horrible death of hydrophobia without wishing "to exile man's best ideal of fidelity from the hearthstones of civilization." If we must have an "ideal of fidelity" why not find it, not in the dog that kills the child, but in the father that kills the dog. The profit of maintaining a standard and pattern of the virtues (at considerable expense in the case of this insatiable canine consumer) may be great, but are we so hard pushed that we must go to the animals for it? In life and letters are there no men and women whose names kindle enthusiasm and emulation? Is fidelity, is devotion, is self-sacrifice unknown among ourselves? As a model of the higher virtues why will not one's mother serve at a pinch? And what is the matter with Miss Guiney herself? She is faithful, at least to dogs, whatever she may be to the hundreds of American children inevitably foredoomed to a death of unthinkable agony.

There is perhaps a hope that when the sun's returning flame shall gild the hither end of the thirtieth century this savage and filthy brute, the dog, will have ceased to "banquet on through a whole year" of human fat and lean; that he will have been gathered to his variously unworthy fathers to give an account of the deeds done in body of man. In the meantime, those of us who have not the enlightened understanding to be enamored of him may endure with such fortitude as we can command his feats of tooth among the shins and throats of those who have; we ourselves are so few that there is a strong numerical presumption of personal immunity.

It is well to have a clear understanding of such inconveniences as may be expected to ensue from dog-bites. That inconveniences and even discomforts do sometimes flow from, or at least follow, the mischance of being bitten by dogs, even the sturdiest champion of "man's best friend" will admit when not heated fay controversy. True, he is disposed to sympathy for those incurring the inconveniences and discomforts, but against apparent incompassion may be offset his indubitable sympathy with the dog. No one is altogether heartless.

Amongst the several disadvantages of a close personal connection with the canine tooth, the disorder known as hydrophobia has long held an undisputed primacy. The existence of dus ailment is attested by so many witnesses, many of whom, belonging to the profession of medicine, speak with a certain authority, that even the breeders and lovers of snap-dogs are compelled reluctantly to concede it, though as a rule they stoutly deny that it is imparted by the dog. In their view, hydrophobia is a theory, not a condition. The patient imagines himself to have it, and acting upon that unsupported assumption or hypothesis, suffers and dies in the attempt to square his conduct with his opinions.

It seems there is firmer ground for their view of the matter than the rest of us have been willing to admit There is such a thing, doubtless, as hydrophobia proper, but also there is such another thing as pseudo-hydrophobia, or hydrophobia improper.

Pseudo-hydrophobia, the physicians explain, is caused by fear of hydrophobia.

The patient, having been chewed by a healthy and harmless dog, broods upon his imaginary peril, solicitously watches his imaginary symptoms, and, finally, persuading himself of their reality, puts them on exhibition, as he understands them. He runs about (when permitted) on his hands and knees, growls, barks, howls, and in default of a tail wags the part of him where it would be if he had one. In a few days he is gone before, a victim to his lack of confidence in man's best friend.

The number of cases of pseudo-hydrophobia, relatively, to those of true hydrophobia, is not definitely known, the medical records having been imperfectly made, and never collated; champions of the snap-dog, as intimated, believe it is many to nothing. That being so (they argue), the animal is entirely exonerated, and leaves the discussion without a stain upon his reputation.

But that is feeble reasoning. Even if we grant their premises we can not embrace their conclusion. In the first place, it hurts to be bitten by a dog, as the dog himself audibly confesses when bitten by another dog. Furthermore, pseudo-hydrophobia is quite as fatal as if it were a legitimate product of the bite, not a result of the terror which that mischance inspires.

Human nature being what it is, and well known to the dog to be what it is, we have a right to expect that the creature will take our weaknesses into consideration--that he will respect our addiction to reasonless panic, even as we respect his when, as we commonly do, we refrain from attaching tinware to his tail. A dog that runs himself to death to evade a kitchen utensil which could not possibly harm him, and which if he did not flee would not pursue, is the author of his own undoing in precisely the same sense as is the victim of pseudo-hydrophobia. He is slain by a theory, not a condition. Yet the wicked boy that set him going is not blameless, and no one would be so zealous and strenuous in his prosecution as the cynolater, the adorer of dogs, the person who holds them guileless of pseudo-hydrophobia.

Mr. Nicholas Smith, while United States Consul at Liege, wrote, or caused to be written, an official report, wickedly, willfully and maliciously designed to abridge the privileges, augment the ills and impair the honorable status of the domestic dog. In the very beginning of this report Mr. Smith manifests his animus by stigmatizing the domestic dog as an "hereditary loafer;" and having hurled the allegation, affirms "the dawn of a [Belgian] new era" wherein the pampered menial will loaf no more. There is to be no more sun-soaking on door mats having a southern exposure, no more usurpation of the warmest segment of the family circle, no more successful personal solicitation of cheer at the domestic board. The dog's place in the social scale is no longer to be determined by consideration of sentiment, but will be the result of cold commercial calculation, and so fixed as best to serve the ends of industrial expediency. All this in Belgium, where the dog is already in active service as a beast of burden and draught; doubtless the transition to that humble condition from his present and immemorial social elevation in less advanced countries will be slow and characterized by bitter factional strife. America, especially, though ever accessible to the infection of new and profitable ideas, will be angularly slow to accept so radical a subversion of a social superstructure that almost may be said to rest upon the domestic dog as a basic verity.

The dogs are our only true "leisure class" (for even the tramps are sometimes compelled to engage in such simple industries as are possible within the "precincts" of the county jail) and we are justly proud of them. They toil not, neither spin, yet Solomon in all his glory was not a dog. Instead of making them hewers of wood and drawers of water, it would be more consonant with the Anglomaniacal and general Old World spirit, now so dominant in the councils of the nation, to make them "hereditary legislators." And Mr. Smith must permit me to add, with a special significance, that history records an instance of even a horse making a fairly good Consul.

Mr. Smith avers with obvious and impudent satisfaction that in Liege twice as many draught dogs as horses are seen in the streets, attached to vehicles. He regards "a gaily painted cart" drawn by "a well fed dog" and driven by a well fed (and gaily painted) woman as a "pleasing vision." I do not; I should prefer to see the dog sitting at the receipt of steaks and chops and the lady devoting herself to the amelioration of the condition of the universe, and the manufacture of poetry and stories that are not true. A more pleasing vision, too, one endeared to eye and heart by immemorial use and wont, is that of stranger and dog indulging in the pleasures of the chase-- stranger a little ahead--while the woman in the case manifests a characteristically compassionate solicitude lest the gentleman's trousers do not match Fido's mustache. It is, indeed, impossible to regard with any degree of approval the degradation to commercial utility of two so noble animals as Dog and Woman; and if Man had joined them together by driving-reins I should hope that God would put them asunder, even if the reins were held by Dog. There would no doubt be a distinct gain as well as a certain artistic fitness in unyoking the strong-minded female of our species from the Chariot of Progress and yoking her to the apple-cart or fish-wagon, and--but that is another story; the imminence of the draughtwoman is not foreshadowed in the report of our Consul at Liege.

Mr. Smith's estimate of the number of dogs in this country at 7,000,000 is a "conservative" one, it must be confessed, and can hardly have been based on observations by moonlight in a suburban village; his estimate of the effective strength of the average dog at 500 pounds is probably about right, as will be attested by any intelligent boy who in campaigns against orchards has experienced detention by the Cerberi of the places. Taking his own figures Mr. Smith calculates that we have in this country 3,500,000,000 pounds of "idle dog power." But this statement is more ingenious than ingenuous; it gives, as doubtless it was intended to give, the impression that we have only idle dogs, whereas of all mundane forces the domestic dog is most easily stirred to action. His expense of energy in pursuit of the harmless, necessary flea, for example, is prodigious; and he is not infrequently seen in chase of his own tail, with an activity scarcely inferior. If there is anything worth while in accepted theories of the conversion and conservation of force these gigantic energies are by no means wasted; they appear as heat, light and electricity, modifying climate, reducing gas bills and assisting in propulsion of street cars. Even in baying the moon and insulting visitors and bypassers the dog releases a certain amount of vibratory force which through various mutations of its wave-length, may do its part in cooking a steak or gratifying the olfactory nerve by throwing fresh perfume on the violet. Evidently the commercial advantages of deposing the dog from the position of Exalted Personage and subduing him to that of Motor would not be all clear gain. He would no longer have the spirit to send, Whitmanwise, his barbarous but beneficent yawp over the housetops, nor the leisure to throw off vast quantities of energy by centrifugal efforts at the conquest of his tail. As to the fleas, he would accept them with apathetic satisfaction as preventives of thought upon his fallen fortunes.

Having observed with attention and considered with seriousness the London *Daily News* declares its conviction that the dog, as we have the happiness to know him, is dreadfully bored by civilization. This is one of the gravest accusations that the friends of progress and light have been called out to meet--a challenge that it is impossible to ignore and unprofitable to evade; for the dog as we have the happiness to know him is the only dog that we have the happiness really to know. The wolf is hardly a dog within the meaning of the law, nor is the scalp-yielding coyote, whether he howls or merely sings and plays the piano; moreover, these are beyond the pale of civilization and outside the scope of our sympathies.

With the dog it is different His place is among us; he is with us and of us--a part of our life and love. If we are maintaining and promoting a condition of things that gives him "that tired feeling" it is befitting that we mend our ways lest, shaking the carpet dust from his feet and the tenderloin steaks from his teeth, he depart from our midst and connect himself with the enchanted life of the thrilling barbarian. We can not afford to lose him. The cynophobes may call him a "survival" and sneer at his exhausted mandate--albeit, as Darwin points out, they are indebted for their sneer to his own habit of uncovering his teeth to bite; they may seek to cast opprobrium upon the nature of our affection for him by pronouncing it hereditary--a bequest from our primitive ancestors, for whom he performed important service in other ways than depriving visitors of their tendons; but quite the same we should miss him at his meal time and in the (but for him) silent watches of the night. We should miss his bark and his bite, the feel of his forefeet upon our shirt-fronts, the frou-frou of his dusty sides against our nether habiliments. More than all, we should miss and mourn that visible yearning for chops and steaks, which he has persuaded us to accept as the lovelight of his eye and a tribute to our personal worth. We must keep the dog, and to that end find means to abate his weariness of us and our ways.

Doubtless much might be done to reclaim our dogs from their uncheerful state of mind by abstention from debate on imperialism; by excluding them from the churches, at least during the sermons; by keeping them off the streets and out of hearing when rites of prostration are in performance before visiting notables; by forbidding anyone to read aloud in their hearing the sensational articles in the newspapers, and by educating them to the belief that Labor and Capital are illusions. A limitation of the annual output of popular novels would undoubtedly reduce the dejection, which could be still further mitigated by abolition of the more successful magazines. If the dialect story or poem could be prohibited, under severe penalties, the sum of night-howling (erroneously attributed to lunar influence) would experience an audible decrement, which, also, would enable the fire department to augment its own uproar without reproach. There is, indeed, a considerable number of ways in which we might effect a double reform--promoting the advantage of Man, as well as medicating the mental fatigue of Dog. For another example, it would be "a boon and a blessing to man" if Society would put to death, or at least banish, the mill-man or manufacturer who persists in apprising the entire community many times a day by means of a steam whistle that it is time for his oppressed employees (every one of whom has a gold watch) to go to work or to leave off. Such things not only make a dog tired, they make a man mad. They answer with an accented affirmative Truthful James' plaintive inquiry,

"Is civilization a failure,
Or is the Caucasian played out?"

Unquestionably, from his advantageous point of view as a looker-on at the game, the dog is justified in the conviction that they are.

THE ANCESTRAL BOND

A WELL-KNOWN citizen of Ohio once discovered another man of the same name exactly resembling him, and writing a "hand" which, including the signature, he was unable to distinguish from his own. The two men were unable to discover any blood relationship between them. It is nevertheless almost absolutely certain that a relationship existed, though it may have been so remote a degree that the familiar term "forty-second cousin" would not have exaggerated the slenderness of the tie. The phenomena of heredity have been inattentively noted; its laws are imperfectly understood, even by Herbert Spencer and the prophets. My own small study in this amazing field convinces me that a man is the sum of his ancestors; that his character, moral and intellectual, is determined before his birth. His environment with all its varied suasions, its agencies of good and evil; breeding, training, interest, experience and the rest of it--have little to do with the matter and can not alter the sentence passed upon him at conception, compelling him to be what he is.

Man is the hither end of an immeasurable line extending back to the ultimate Adam--or, as we scientists prefer to name him, Protoplasmos. Man travels, not the mental road that he would, but the one that he must--is pushed this way and that by the resultant of all the forces behind him; for each member of the ancestral line, though dead, yet pusfaedi. In one of what Dr. Nolmes (Holmes, ed.) calls his "medicated novels," *The Guardian Angel*, this truth is most admirably and lucidly set forth with abundant instance and copious exposition. Upon another work of his, *Elsie Venner*--in which he erroneously affirms the influence of circumstance and environment--let us lay a charitable hand and fling it into the fire.

Clearly all one's ancestors have not equal power in shaping his character. Conceiving them, according to our figure, as arranged in line behind him and influential in the ratio of their individuality, we shall get the best notion of their method by supposing them to have taken their places in an order somewhat independent of chronology and a little different from their arrangement behind his brother. Immediately at his back, with a controlling hand (a trifle skinny) upon him, may stand his great-grandmother, while his father may be many removes arear. Or the place of power may be held by some fine old Asian gentleman who flourished before the confusion of tongues on the plain of Shinar; or by some cave-dweller who polished the bone of life in Mesopotamia and was perhaps a respectable and honest troglodyte.

Sometimes a whole platoon of ancestors appears to have been moved backward or forward, *en bloc* not, we may be sure, capriciously, but in obedience to some law that we do not understand. I know a man to whose character not an ancestor since the seventeenth century has contributed an element. Intellectually he is a contemporary of John Dryden, whom naturally he reveres as the greatest of poets. I know another who has inherited his handwriting from his great-grandfather, although he has been trained to the Spencerian system and tried hard to acquire it. Furthermore, his handwriting follows the same order of progressive development as that of his greatgrandfather. At the age of twenty he wrote exactly as his ancestor did at the same age, and, although at forty-five his chirography is nothing like what it was even ten years ago, it is accurately like his great-grandfather's at forty-five. It was only five years ago that the discovery of some old letters showed him how his great-grandfather wrote, and accounted for the absolute dissimilarity of his own handwriting to that of any known member of his family.

To suppose that such individual traits as the configuration of the body, the color of the hair and eyes, the shape of hands and feet, the thousand-and-one subtle characteristics that make family resemblances are transmissible, and that the form, texture and capacities of the brain which fix the degree of natural intellect, are ***not*** transmissible, is illogical and absurd. We see that certain actions, such as gestures, gait, and so forth, resulting from the most complex concurrences of brain, nerves and muscles, are hereditary. Is it reasonable to suppose that the brain alone of all the organs performs its work according to its own sweet will, free from congenital tendencies? Is it not a familiar fact that racial characteristics are persistent?--that one race is stupid and indocile, another quick and intelligent? Does not each generation of a race inherit the intellectual qualities of the preceding generation? How could this be true of generations and not of individuals?

As to stirpiculture, the intelligent and systematic breeding of men and women with a view to improvement of the species--it is a thing of the far future, It is hardly in sight. Yet, what splendid possibilities it carries! Two or three generations of as careful breeding as we bestow on horses, dogs and pigeons would do more good than all the penal, reformatory and educating agencies of the world accomplish in a thousand years. It is the one direction in which human effort to "elevate the race" can be assured of a definitive, speedy and adequate success. It is hardly better than nonsense to prate of any good coming to the race through (for example) medical science, which is mainly concerned in reversing the beneficent operation of natural laws and saving the unfittest to perpetuate their unfitness. Our entire system of charities is of, to the same objection; it cares for the incapables whom Nature is trying to "weed out," This not only debases the race physically, intellectually and morally, but constantly increases the rate of debasement. The proportion of criminals, paupers and the various kinds of "inmates" of charitable institutions augments its horrible percentage yearly. On the other hand, our wars destroy the capable; so thus we make inroads upon the vitality of the race from two directions. We preserve the feeble and extirpate the strong. He who, in view of this amazing folly can believe in a constant, even slow, progress of the human race toward perfection ought to be happy. He has a mind whose Olympian heights are inaccessible--the

Titans of fact can never scale them to storm its ancient reign.

THE RIGHT TO WORK

ALL kinds of relief, charitable or other, doubtless tend to perpetuation of pauperism, inasmuch as paupers are thereby kept alive; and living paupers unquestionably propagate their unthrifty kind more abundantly than dead ones. It is not true, though, that relief interferes with Nature's beneficent law of the survival of the fittest, for the power to excite sympathy and obtain relief is a kind of fitness. I am still a devotee of the homely primitive doctrine that mischance, disability or even unthrift, is not a capital crime justly and profitably punishable by starvation. I still regard the Good Samaritan with a certain toleration and Jesus Christ's tenderness to the poor as something more than a policy of obstruction.

If no such thing as an almshouse, a hospital, an asylum or any one of the many public establishments for relief of the unfortunate were known the proposal to found one would indubitably evoke from thousands of throats notes of deprecation and predictions of disaster. It would be called Socialism of the radical and dangerous kind--of a kind to menace the stability of government and undermine the very foundations of organized society! Yet who is more truly unfortunate than an able-bodied man out of work through no delinquency of will and no default of effort? Is hunger to him and his less poignant than to the feeble in body and mind whom we support for nothing in almshouse or asylum? Are cold and exposure less disagreeable to him than to them? Is not his claim to the right to live as valid as theirs if backed by the will to pay for life with work? And in denial of his claim is there not latent a far greater peril to society than inheres in denial of theirs? So unfortunate and dangerous a creature as a man willing to work, yet having no work to do, should be unknown outside of the literature of satire. Doubtless there would be enormous difficulties in devising a practicable and beneficent system, and doubtless the reform, like all permanent and salutary reforms, will have to grow. The growth naturally will be delayed by opposition of the workingmen themselves--precisely as they oppose prison labor from ignorance that labor makes labor.

It matters not that nine in ten of all our tramps and vagrants are such from choice, and irreclaimable degenerates into the bargain; so long as one worthy man is out of employment and unable to obtain it our duty is to provide it by law. Nay, so long as industrial conditions are such that so pathetic a phenomenon is possible we have not the moral right to disregard that possibility. The right to employment being the right to life, its denial is homicide. It should be needless to point out the advantages of its concession. It would preserve the life and self-respect of him who is needy through misfortune, and supply an infallible means of detection of his criminal imitator, who could then be dealt with as he deserves, widiout the lenity that finds justification in doubt and compassion. It would diminish crime, for an empty stomach has no morals. With a wage rate lower than the commercial, it would disturb no private industries by luring away their workmen, and with nothing made to sell there would be no competition with private products. Properly directed, it would give us highways, bridges and embankments which we shall not otherwise have.

It is difficult to say if our laws relating to vagrancy and vagrants are more cruel or more absurd. If not so atrocious they would evoke laughter; if less ridiculous we should read them with indignation. Here is an imaginary conversation:

The Law: It is forbidden to you to rob. It is forbidden to you to steal. It is forbidden to you to beg.

The Vagrant: Being without money, and denied employment, I am compelled to obtain food, shelter and clothing in one of these ways, else I shall be hungry and cold.

The Law: That is no affair of mine. Yet I am considerate--you are permitted to be as hungry as you like and as cold as may suit you.

The Vagrant: Hungry, yes, and many thanks to you; but if I go naked I am arrested for indecent exposure. You require me to wear clothing.

The Law: You'll admit that you need it.

The Vagrant: But not that you provide a way for me to get it. No one will give me shelter at night; you forbid me to sleep in a straw stack.

The Law: Ungrateful man! we provide a cell.

The Vagrant: Even when I obey you, starving all day and freezing all night, and holding my tongue with both hands, I am liable to arrest for being "without visible means of support."

The Law: A most reprehensible condition.

The Vagrant: One thing has been overlooked--a legal punishment for begging for work.

The Law: True; I am not perfect.

THE RIGHT TO TAKE ONESELF OFF

A PERSON who loses heart and hope through a personal bereavement is like a grain of sand on the seashore complaining that the tide has washed a neighboring grain out of reach. He is worse, for the bereaved grain cannot help itself; it has to be a grain of sand and play the game of tide, win or lose; whereas he can quit--by watching his opportunity can "quit a winner." For sometimes we do beat "the man who keeps the table"--never in the long run, but infrequently and out of small stakes. But this is no time to "cash in" and go, for you can not take your little winning with you. The time to quit is when you have lost a big stake, your fool hope of eventual success, your fortitude and your love of the game. If you stay in the game, which you are not compelled to do, take your losses in good temper and do not whine about them. They are hard to bear, but that is no reason why you should be.

But we are told with tiresome iteration that we are "put here" for some purpose (not disclosed) and have no right to retire until summoned--it may be by small-pox, it may be by the bludgeon of a blackguard, it may be by the kick of a cow; the "summoning" Power (said to be the same as the "putting" Power) has not a nice taste in the choice of messengers. That "argument" is not worth attention, for it is unsupported by either evidence or anything remotely resembling evidence. "Put here." Indeed! And by the keeper of the table who "runs" the "skin game." We were put here by our parents--that is all anybody knows about it; and they had no more authority than we, and probably no more intention.

The notion that we have not the right to take our own lives comes of our consciousness that we have not the courage. It is the plea of the coward--his excuse for continuing to live when he has nothing to live for--or his provision against such a time in the future. If he were not egotist as well as coward he would need no excuse. To one who does not regard himself as the center of creation and his sorrow as the throes of the universe, life, if not worth living, is also not worth leaving. The ancient philosopher who was asked why he did not the if, as he taught, life was no better than death, replied: "Because death is no better than life." We do not know that either proposition is true, but the matter is not worth bothering about, for both states are supportable--life despite its pleasures and death despite its repose.

It was Robert G. Ingersoll's opinion that there is rather too little than too much suicide in the world--that people are so cowardly as to live on long after endurance has ceased to be a virtue. This view is but a return to the wisdom of the ancients, in whose splendid civilization suicide had as honorable place as any other courageous, reasonable and unselfish act. Antony, Brutus, Cato, Seneca--these were not of the kind of men to do deeds of cowardice and folly. The smug, self-righteous modern way of looking upon the act as that of a craven or a lunatic is the creation of priests, Philistines and women. If courage is manifest in endurance of profitless discomfort it is cowardice to warm oneself when cold, to cure oneself when ill, to drive away mosquitoes, to go in when it rains. The "pursuit of happiness," then, is not an "inalienable right," for that implies avoidance of pain. No principle is involved in this matter; suicide is justifiable or not, according to circumstances; each case is to be considered on its merits and he having the act under advisement is sole judge. To his decision, made with whatever light he may chance to have, all honest minds will bow. The appellant has no court to which to take his appeal. Nowhere is a jurisdiction so comprehensive as to embrace the right of condemning the wretched to life.

Suicide is always courageous. We call it courage in a soldier merely to face death--say to lead a forlorn hope--although he has a chance of life and a certainty of "glory." But the suicide does more than face death; he incurs it, and with a certainty, not of glory, but of reproach. If that is not courage we must reform our vocabulary.

True, there may be a higher courage in living than in dying--a moral courage greater than physical. The courage of the suicide, like that of the pirate, is not incompatible with a selfish disregard of the rights and interests of others--a cruel recreancy to duty and decency. I have been asked: "Do you not think it cowardly when a man leaves his family unprovided for, to end his life, because he is dissatisfied with life in general?" No, I do not; I think it selfish and cruel. Is not that enough to say of it? Must we distort words from their true meaning in order more effectually to damn the act and cover its author with a greater infamy? A word means something; despite the maunderings of the lexicographers, it does not mean whatever you want it to mean. "Cowardice" means the fear of danger, not the shirking of duty. The writer who allows himself as much liberty in the use of words as he is allowed by the dictionary-maker and by popular consent is a bad writer. He can make no impression on his reader, and would do better service at the ribbon-counter.

The ethics of suicide is not a simple matter; one can not lay down laws of universal application, but each case is to be judged, if judged at all, with a full knowledge of all the circumstances, including the mental and moral make-up of the person taking his own life--an impossible qualification for judgment. One's time, race and religion have much to do with it. Some people, like the ancient Romans and the modern Japanese, have considered suicide in certain circumstances honorable and obligatory; among ourselves it is held in disfavor. A man of sense will not give much attention to considerations of that kind, excepting in so far as they affect others, but in judging weak offenders they are to be taken into the account. Speaking generally, then, I should say that in our time and country the following persons (and some others) are justified in removing themselves, and that to some of them it is a duty:

One afflicted with a painful or loathsome and incurable disease.

One who is a heavy burden to his friends, with no prospect of their relief.

One threatened with permanent insanity.

One irreclaimably addicted to drunkenness or some similarly destructive or offensive habit.

One without friends, property, employment or hope.

One who has disgraced himself.

Why do we honor the valiant soldier, sailor, fireman? For obedience to duty? Not at all; that alone--without the peril--seldom elicits remark, never evokes enthusiasm. It is because he faced without flinching the risk of that supreme disaster--or what we feel to be such--death. But look you: the soldier braves the danger of death; the suicide braves death itself! The leader of the forlorn hope may not be struck. The sailor who voluntarily goes down with his ship may be picked up or cast ashore. It is not certain that the wall will topple until the fireman shall have descended with his precious burden. But the suicide--his is the foeman that never missed a mark, his the sea that gives nothing back; the wall that he mounts bears no man's weight And his, at the end of it all, is the dishonored grave where the wild ass of public opinion

"Stamps o'er his head but can not break his sleep."

The Codes Of Hammurabi And Moses
W. W. Davies

QTY

The discovery of the Hammurabi Code is one of the greatest achievements of archaeology, and is of paramount interest, not only to the student of the Bible, but also to all those interested in ancient history...

Religion   **ISBN:** *1-59462-338-4*   **Pages:132**
MSRP $12.95

The Theory of Moral Sentiments
Adam Smith

QTY

This work from 1749. contains original theories of conscience amd moral judgment and it is the foundation for systemof morals.

Philosophy   **ISBN:** *1-59462-777-0*   **Pages:536**
MSRP $19.95

Jessica's First Prayer
Hesba Stretton

QTY

In a screened and secluded corner of one of the many railway-bridges which span the streets of London there could be seen a few years ago, from five o'clock every morning until half past eight, a tidily set-out coffee-stall, consisting of a trestle and board, upon which stood two large tin cans, with a small fire of charcoal burning under each so as to keep the coffee boiling during the early hours of the morning when the work-people were thronging into the city on their way to their daily toil...

Childrens   **ISBN:** *1-59462-373-2*   **Pages:84**
MSRP $9.95

My Life and Work
Henry Ford

QTY

Henry Ford revolutionized the world with his implementation of mass production for the Model T automobile. Gain valuable business insight into his life and work with his own auto-biography... "We have only started on our development of our country we have not as yet, with all our talk of wonderful progress, done more than scratch the surface. The progress has been wonderful enough but..."

Biographies/   **ISBN:** *1-59462-198-5*   **Pages:300**
MSRP $21.95

The Art of Cross-Examination
Francis Wellman

QTY

I presume it is the experience of every author, after his first book is published upon an important subject, to be almost overwhelmed with a wealth of ideas and illustrations which could readily have been included in his book, and which to his own mind, at least, seem to make a second edition inevitable. Such certainly was the case with me; and when the first edition had reached its sixth impression in five months, I rejoiced to learn that it seemed to my publishers that the book had met with a sufficiently favorable reception to justify a second and considerably enlarged edition. ..

Pages:412

Reference   ISBN: *1-59462-647-2*   *MSRP $19.95*

On the Duty of Civil Disobedience
Henry David Thoreau

QTY

Thoreau wrote his famous essay, On the Duty of Civil Disobedience, as a protest against an unjust but popular war and the immoral but popular institution of slave-owning. He did more than write—he declined to pay his taxes, and was hauled off to gaol in consequence. Who can say how much this refusal of his hastened the end of the war and of slavery ?

Law   ISBN: *1-59462-747-9*   **Pages:48**

MSRP $7.45

Dream Psychology Psychoanalysis for Beginners
Sigmund Freud

QTY

Sigmund Freud, born Sigismund Schlomo Freud (May 6, 1856 - September 23, 1939), was a Jewish-Austrian neurologist and psychiatrist who co-founded the psychoanalytic school of psychology. Freud is best known for his theories of the unconscious mind, especially involving the mechanism of repression; his redefinition of sexual desire as mobile and directed towards a wide variety of objects; and his therapeutic techniques, especially his understanding of transference in the therapeutic relationship and the presumed value of dreams as sources of insight into unconscious desires.

Pages:196

Psychology   ISBN: *1-59462-905-6*   *MSRP $15.45*

The Miracle of Right Thought
Orison Swett Marden

QTY

Believe with all of your heart that you will do what you were made to do. When the mind has once formed the habit of holding cheerful, happy, prosperous pictures, it will not be easy to form the opposite habit. It does not matter how improbable or how far away this realization may see, or how dark the prospects may be, if we visualize them as best we can, as vividly as possible, hold tenaciously to them and vigorously struggle to attain them, they will gradually become actualized, realized in the life. But a desire, a longing without endeavor, a yearning abandoned or held indifferently will vanish without realization.

Pages:360

Self Help   ISBN: *1-59462-644-8*   *MSRP $25.45*

QTY

The Rosicrucian Cosmo-Conception Mystic Christianity *by Max Heindel*   ISBN: *1-59462-188-8*   **$38.95**
The Rosicrucian Cosmo-conception is not dogmatic, neither does it appeal to any other authority than the reason of the student. It is: not controversial, but is: sent forth in the, hope that it may help to clear...   New Age/Religion Pages 646

Abandonment To Divine Providence *by Jean-Pierre de Caussade*   ISBN: *1-59462-228-0*   **$25.95**
"The Rev. Jean Pierre de Caussade was one of the most remarkable spiritual writers of the Society of Jesus in France in the 18th Century. His death took place at Toulouse in 1751. His works have gone through many editions and have been republished...   Inspirational/Religion Pages 400

Mental Chemistry *by Charles Haanel*   ISBN: *1-59462-192-6*   **$23.95**
Mental Chemistry allows the change of material conditions by combining and appropriately utilizing the power of the mind. Much like applied chemistry creates something new and unique out of careful combinations of chemicals the mastery of mental chemistry...   New Age Pages 354

The Letters of Robert Browning and Elizabeth Barret Barrett 1845-1846 vol II   ISBN: *1-59462-193-4*   **$35.95**
by Robert Browning and Elizabeth Barrett   Biographies Pages 596

Gleanings In Genesis (volume I) *by Arthur W. Pink*   ISBN: *1-59462-130-6*   **$27.45**
Appropriately has Genesis been termed "the seed plot of the Bible" for in it we have, in germ form, almost all of the great doctrines which are afterwards fully developed in the books of Scripture which follow...   Religion/Inspirational Pages 420

The Master Key *by L. W. de Laurence*   ISBN: *1-59462-001-6*   **$30.95**
In no branch of human knowledge has there been a more lively increase of the spirit of research during the past few years than in the study of Psychology, Concentration and Mental Discipline. The requests for authentic lessons in Thought Control, Mental Discipline and...   New Age/Business Pages 422

The Lesser Key Of Solomon Goetia *by L. W. de Laurence*   ISBN: *1-59462-092-X*   **$9.95**
This translation of the first book of the "Lernegton" which is now for the first time made accessible to students of Talismanic Magic was done, after careful collation and edition, from numerous Ancient Manuscripts in Hebrew, Latin, and French...   New Age/Occult Pages 92

Rubaiyat Of Omar Khayyam *by Edward Fitzgerald*   ISBN:*1-59462-332-5*   **$13.95**
Edward Fitzgerald, whom the world has already learned, in spite of his own efforts to remain within the shadow of anonymity, to look upon as one of the rarest poets of the century, was born at Bredfield, in Suffolk, on the 31st of March, 1809. He was the third son of John Purcell...   Music Pages 172

Ancient Law *by Henry Maine*   ISBN: *1-59462-128-4*   **$29.95**
The chief object of the following pages is to indicate some of the earliest ideas of mankind, as they are reflected in Ancient Law, and to point out the relation of those ideas to modern thought.   Religiom/History Pages 452

Far-Away Stories *by William J. Locke*   ISBN: *1-59462-129-2*   **$19.45**
"Good wine needs no bush, but a collection of mixed vintages does. And this book is just such a collection. Some of the stories I do not want to remain buried for ever in the museum files of dead magazine-numbers an author's not unpardonable vanity..."   Fiction Pages 272

Life of David Crockett *by David Crockett*   ISBN: *1-59462-250-7*   **$27.45**
"Colonel David Crockett was one of the most remarkable men of the times in which he lived. Born in humble life, but gifted with a strong will, an indomitable courage, and unremitting perseverance...   Biographies/New Age Pages 424

Lip-Reading *by Edward Nitchie*   ISBN: *1-59462-206-X*   **$25.95**
Edward B. Nitchie, founder of the New York School for the Hard of Hearing, now the Nitchie School of Lip-Reading, Inc, wrote "LIP-READING Principles and Practice". The development and perfecting of this meritorious work on lip-reading was an undertaking...   How-to Pages 400

A Handbook of Suggestive Therapeutics, Applied Hypnotism, Psychic Science   ISBN: *1-59462-214-0*   **$24.95**
by Henry Munro   Health/New Age/Health/Self-help Pages 376

A Doll's House: and Two Other Plays *by Henrik Ibsen*   ISBN: *1-59462-112-8*   **$19.95**
Henrik Ibsen created this classic when in revolutionary 1848 Rome. Introducing some striking concepts in playwriting for the realist genre, this play has been studied the world over.   Fiction/Classics/Plays 308

The Light of Asia *by sir Edwin Arnold*   ISBN: *1-59462-204-3*   **$13.95**
In this poetic masterpiece, Edwin Arnold describes the life and teachings of Buddha. The man who was to become known as Buddha to the world was born as Prince Gautama of India but he rejected the worldly riches and abandoned the reigns of power when...   Religion/History/Biographies Pages 170

The Complete Works of Guy de Maupassant *by Guy de Maupassant*   ISBN: *1-59462-157-8*   **$16.95**
"For days and days, nights and nights, I had dreamed of that first kiss which was to consecrate our engagement, and I knew not on what spot I should put my lips..."   Fiction/Classics Pages 240

The Art of Cross-Examination *by Francis L. Wellman*   ISBN: *1-59462-309-0*   **$26.95**
Written by a renowned trial lawyer, Wellman imparts his experience and uses case studies to explain how to use psychology to extract desired information through questioning.   How-to/Science/Reference Pages 408

Answered or Unanswered? *by Louisa Vaughan*   ISBN: *1-59462-248-5*   **$10.95**
Miracles of Faith in China   Religion Pages 112

The Edinburgh Lectures on Mental Science (1909) *by Thomas*   ISBN: *1-59462-008-3*   **$11.95**
This book contains the substance of a course of lectures recently given by the writer in the Queen Street Hail, Edinburgh. Its purpose is to indicate the Natural Principles governing the relation between Mental Action and Material Conditions...   New Age/Psychology Pages 148

Ayesha *by H. Rider Haggard*   ISBN: *1-59462-301-5*   **$24.95**
Verily and indeed it is the unexpected that happens! Probably if there was one person upon the earth from whom the Editor of this, and of a certain previ-ous history, did not expect to hear again...   Classics Pages 380

Ayala's Angel *by Anthony Trollope*   ISBN: *1-59462-352-X*   **$29.95**
The two girls were both pretty, but Lucy who was twenty-one who supposed to be simple and comparatively unattractive, whereas Ayala was credited, as her Bombwhat romantic name might show, with poetic charm and a taste for romance. Ayala when her father died was nineteen...   Fiction Pages 484

The American Commonwealth *by James Bryce*   ISBN: *1-59462-286-8*   **$34.45**
An interpretation of American democratic political theory. It examines political mechanics and society from the perspective of Scotsman James Bryce   Politics Pages 572

Stories of the Pilgrims *by Margaret P. Pumphrey*   ISBN: *1-59462-116-0*   **$17.95**
This book explores pilgrims religious oppression in England as well as their escape to Holland and eventual crossing to America on the Mayflower, and their early days in New England...   History Pages 268

www.bookjungle.com *email: sales@bookjungle.com fax: 630-214-0564 mail: Book Jungle PO Box 2226 Champaign, IL 61825*

QTY

The Fasting Cure *by Sinclair Upton*   ISBN: *1-59462-222-1*   **$13.95**
In the Cosmopolitan Magazine for May, 1910, and in the Contemporary Review (London) for April, 1910, I published an article dealing with my experiences in fasting. I have written a great many magazine articles, but never one which attracted so much attention... New Age/Self Help/Health Pages 164

Hebrew Astrology *by Sepharial*   ISBN: *1-59462-308-2*   **$13.45**
In these days of advanced thinking it is a matter of common observation that we have left many of the old landmarks behind and that we are now pressing forward to greater heights and to a wider horizon than that which represented the mind-content of our progenitors... Astrology Pages 144

Thought Vibration or The Law of Attraction in the Thought World   ISBN: *1-59462-127-6*   **$12.95**
by William Walker Atkinson   *Psychology/Religion Pages 144*

Optimism *by Helen Keller*   ISBN: *1-59462-108-X*   **$15.95**
Helen Keller was blind, deaf, and mute since 19 months old, yet famously learned how to overcome these handicaps, communicate with the world, and spread her lectures promoting optimism. An inspiring read for everyone... Biographies/Inspirational Pages 84

Sara Crewe *by Frances Burnett*   ISBN: *1-59462-360-0*   **$9.45**
In the first place, Miss Minchin lived in London. Her home was a large, dull, tall one, in a large, dull square, where all the houses were alike, and all the sparrows were alike, and where all the door-knockers made the same heavy sound... Childrens/Classic Pages 88

The Autobiography of Benjamin Franklin *by Benjamin Franklin*   ISBN: *1-59462-135-7*   **$24.95**
The Autobiography of Benjamin Franklin has probably been more extensively read than any other American historical work, and no other book of its kind has had such ups and downs of fortune. Franklin lived for many years in England, where he was agent... Biographies/History Pages 332

Name	
Email	
Telephone	
Address	
City, State ZIP	

☐ **Credit Card**   ☐ **Check / Money Order**

Credit Card Number	
Expiration Date	
Signature	

Please Mail to: Book Jungle
PO Box 2226
Champaign, IL 61825
or Fax to: 630-214-0564

ORDERING INFORMATION

web: *www.bookjungle.com*
email: *sales@bookjungle.com*
fax: *630-214-0564*
mail: *Book Jungle PO Box 2226 Champaign, IL 61825*
or PayPal *to sales@bookjungle.com*

Please contact us for bulk discounts

DIRECT-ORDER TERMS

**20% Discount if You Order
Two or More Books**
Free Domestic Shipping!
Accepted: Master Card, Visa,
Discover, American Express

www.ingramcontent.com/pod-product-compliance
Lightning Source LLC
Chambersburg PA
CBHW080824020726
47501CB00009B/2410